MAN WHO NEVER WAS

COLIN NORMAN

The man who never was

Dedication

To my children:
Alison, Anthony, Mike.

I was born when you kissed me,
I died when you left me.
I lived a few weeks while you loved me.
Humphrey Bogart

Preface

From an early age, I craved to write a book, and this book just had to be written. I've always wanted to write something worthwhile for my readers.

I was finally inspired to make a start on my writing three years ago, after my 9-year voluntary involvement at board level in social housing came to an end and I won a national award in the social housing industry. I completed a book called *Reach for the Stars* that alluded to the stars that denoted the organisation competence, which I chaired for five successful years, and that described the journey and work by all involved in a stock transfer of social housing. My book was published by an East Midlands housing group. It was received very well in the trade and garnered many positive reviews on its content. My next project was a book on my experience volunteering for over 47 years. I did this for posterity and called it *A Lifetime's Achievement*. Again, it was well-received. .However, I still had the urge to write fiction, either a novel or novella. My friend, an avid reader, persuaded me to take the plunge, and so I wrote *The Man Who Never Was*.

I was so pleased with the way it flowed out of my head and on to my computer. It is an interesting combination of psychological thriller and love story, with a surprise ending. It is a story worth reading, with the moral being that life does not always go the way we want it too. I do hope you enjoy my story.

C. Norman

PART ONE

CHAPTER 1

Just an idea and a meeting

My story begins in midwinter. My thoughts were turning to a holiday destination for the year ahead. I had reached a point in my career where I had a good position, and I deserved a break from all the problems and management issues, which could easily be delegated to capable colleagues.

We'd had heavy snowfall, and the wind was bitter. The television was not very interesting, and my thoughts turned to my boyhood and early married years, when I enjoyed going to the east coast of England. I had visited the area between King's Lynn and Great Yarmouth, along the coast road, and had discovered many areas and places off the beaten track, as well as on the beaten track. All beautiful and in a world of their own.

As I gazed out of the window and watched the swirling snow, I made up my mind. Usually, I said that I was too busy to have a holiday, but this year would be different, I thought to myself. I had experienced a marriage break-up a couple of years earlier and had not visited the Norfolk area since, so I would arrange a holiday

Before I knew it, the year had changed from January to March. Spring flowers broke through the earth, and the sun began to shine, signalling a new year of growth in the gardens and country lanes. But still I procrastinated, and it wasn't until

May, when the days were longer, and my skin was warmed by the sun, that my mind turned once again to the idea of a holiday. I started organising who would cover my position, someone who I could keep in touch with if needed. There were three people in my consultancy firm that sprang to mind, and Joan seemed to be the best fit to look after both the business and my clients. Joan was more than pleased to oversee things, considering it good for her development, so with that weight off my mind, I could get down to planning my break away.

I had planned to go by car, driving along the coast road and stopping and staying wherever my fancy took me.

June arrived with a vengeance, with heat that we had not seen for years. The weather was perfect for my break. By Friday 15th June, I was all packed and Joan was ready and eager to take the reins. After final stops to the cash-point and petrol station, I was off.

By the time I got to Hunstanton, I needed a breather and so pulled into a roadside café for a slice of toast and a cup of tea. A walk along the seafront, breathing in the bracing sea air, revived me and made me feel that I was finally on holiday.

The seafront was busy with tourists eating ice-cream, children enjoying the sun and freedom, and mums running around after them – a normal seaside scene. I made my way back to the car and decided to drive further along the coast road to find somewhere to stay.

Despite my car's air conditioning, I was soon hot and sticky. Fortunately, it was only half an hour later when I saw a sign for the Whitehouse Hotel. I followed the arrow and found myself on a long drive leading up to an attractive white building. That would suit me!

Having parked the car as near as I could to the entrance, I wheeled my suitcases through the doors. The hotel had a large foyer and reception area, and the whole atmosphere was one of luxury and money. The young lady at reception was thorough and efficient, and within minutes, I had checked into a double room, acquired a key-card and had my cases delivered to my room by a porter.

After a quick wash and brush up, I took the lift down to reception, booked a table for 7 pm, and then went outside to explore the grounds. The grounds were empty, but then most of the hotel guests would still be out for the day. Shrubs and flowers brightened up the mainly grassy areas, and I could see there were many paths to explore. The path I chose led down a slope to a beach that had decent sand, and a few umbrellas with sunbeds underneath. A few women in bikinis sunbathed in their shade. There was very little breeze, and I noticed two yachts moored out to sea. It was the perfect day for sunbathing or having a drink and watching the world go by. White-coated waiters were on hand to fetch and deliver whatever guests required.

I decided to walk along the beach on a path near to the base of the cliffs and came upon stone steps that weren't too steep. These took me into a small car park with a Jaguar parked near a wire fence that had an opening and a road leading from it. My curiosity had me wondering where this road led to, but I decided not to walk along it until I knew more about where it led. Instead, I enjoyed the view over the secluded bay with the two good-sized yachts moored there.

I descended the steps and walked back along the beach, noting that the blond lady on the sun-bed nearest the cliff was very attractive. As I walked past, she turned, lifted her sunglasses and looked at me, smiling, and I was pleased to see that she had a pretty face. I smiled back and nodded at her. I also noticed two men sitting further along the beach. They stood out, for they were not dressed for the beach, with their white shirts, black trousers and matching jackets folded over their arms. The only hint of informality was the addition of dark glasses and the lack of ties. They looked like bodyguards out of a movie.

I took the path back to the hotel. The car park was busier now. Back in my room, I showered and then changed for dinner. I was quick getting ready and so had time to sit on my balcony and take in the scenery. I'm going to enjoy my stay here, I thought as I breathed in the sea air once more. As I surveyed the beach, I could see the two men, but the woman had gone.

Fifteen minutes later, I was at the restaurant waiting for the waiter to find me a table. A combination of a rotary club do and a busy night meant that the restaurant was full and my reservation had been overlooked. In desperation, the head waiter asked if I would mind joining another table. I assured him that I didn't mind at all and then I watched as he walked a few paces to his right and disturbed a couple on the table there. It was the blond woman from the beach with a male companion, and they both nodded their agreement to the waiter.

The waiter came back and escorted me to the table. The man stood, and I introduced myself: "Ray Marriot", shaking his hand. He had a firm grip and was about the same height as me, but very slender. He introduced himself as Bill Stevens, and I turned to his companion, who was giving a smile that would melt any man's heart. Gently, we shook hands, and she introduced herself as Jill. I sat down, wondering why they would want another man's company at their table.

Bill poured me a glass of Chardonnay from the bottle that had been chilling in an ice bucket on the table. I thanked them for allowing me to join them at their table and he said jovially, "We can talk to each other any time, company is good to keep the conversation going."

I watched Jill's face as he said this, and she averted her eyes. I quickly moved the conversation on by asking if they were on holiday and Bill explained that they lived in the house next to the hotel on the cliff top and that they enjoyed coming here some evenings for dinner.

Jill added, "We share the beach adjoining the hotel. I think I noticed you walking on it this afternoon, didn't I?"

"Yes," I replied, "I was exploring the area after having just arrived. I've never been here before."

Another smile, "Oh, I see!"

As she said this, my attention was drawn to a table further along in the corner. Seated at it were the two black-suited men I had seen at the beach.

We ordered our meals from the white-coated waiters. Polite conversation continued through the meal, including mention of a pub along the main road, about 15 miles away, where Bill liked a lunchtime drink and snack. He asked whether I'd like to meet up there sometime, and I agreed that I'd pop in sometime. Jill said that she spent most of her time either sunbathing or shopping in the nearest town.

The mean soon came to an end, and out of the blue Bill asked if he could impose on me to accompany Jill to get some fresh air on a walk around the grounds, something she liked to do following a meal. Surprised, I said I would be delighted to do this, as I enjoyed a short walk after eating. Jill smiled and took my arm. We walked out through the main entrance to the garden area. The night air was not much cooler than the day temperature, and the moon was a full one, so still good light to walk by. The gravel paths also had lamps strategically placed along them.

I suddenly felt unsure of myself, so I started the conversation by asking how long they had lived in the area. Jill explained that they had lived there for about two years, but that Bill had been after the house for a year or two before that. Their house had belonged to his father originally and, after his death, had been sold to cover his debts. Bill was heartbroken at the sale and had vowed to buy it back, which he eventually did. I asked if she had wanted the house as well and whether she liked it. Jill replied that she had only married Bill two years ago on the rebound from a particularly bad marriage to a man she'd known from school days in Coventry. She added, "This time, I married into money and so do not need to work. Bill has two companies in the building trade."

We came to a fork in the path – the left fork led to the beach, and the right fork doubled back to the hotel restaurant. I let Jill decide which way to go, and she decided that it was time to head back. We walked on and, as expected, she asked about my background. I explained that I'd gone through a divorce quite a few years ago and that I had three children who I saw on odd occasions, adding that my ex had remarried. She gave me a smile of sympathy, and I went on to explain that I had thrown myself into my work, starting a new business. The end result of my hard work was ¡a solid business with good clients who kept coming back to us. Unfortunately, I explained ruefully, I had never had time for enjoyment or relaxation, or even a holiday until now.

Jill and I turned the corner into the main hotel car park, and I noticed the Jaguar parked near the entrance. Out of the blue, Jill asked if I was in a relationship at the moment. Surprised, I replied that I was far too busy with work

Bill came out of the hotel doors, "That's good timing. I hope you both enjoyed the walk. We must be off now." He shook my hand, adding, "Maybe I'll see you in the pub tomorrow."

As I bade them farewell, Bill and Jill got in the back of the Jaguar, and the two black-suited men appeared and got in the front. They drove off.

I turned and went into the hotel to my room, my mind full of questions. I knew that my sleep would be disturbed with these questions and mixed feelings. Why would Bill and Jill want company for dinner and why would Bill prefer another man to go for a walk with his wife? Perhaps it was a marriage of convenience. Eventually, I dropped off and slept surprisingly well.

CHAPTER 2

The adventure begins!

I awoke about 6 am. The sun was out, and it was already getting warm. I sat and pondered last night. It seemed strange that the Stevens needed what I now thought were bodyguards. It was unusual for a man to encourage another man, a stranger even, to escort his wife for a walk. But the bodyguards were my biggest puzzle. What danger were they likely to encounter in their home area, and why? My mind was busy trying to analyse it all, but coming to no answer.

When I was ready to go down for breakfast, I decided that I would first ring my PA and ask her to run a check on Bill and Jill. She was a gifted researcher, always able to find out if a business was OK, so I thought she'd be able to get some answers for me. In the meantime, I decided that I was happy to be friends with the couple and enjoy Jill's company.

After breakfast, I went for a walk along the hotel's paths, looking at the shrubs and flowers that were a picture to see this time of the year. There were four gravel paths - the two middle ones went around the garden area, another went to the beach, and the final one went to a car park further back from the one in which I had parked. I walked down the beach path and found Jill already on a sun-bed reading. As I stood, looking around, she looked up, noticed me and waved. I waved back, then turned and headed back up the slope.

I thought this morning I would go down to the town that Bill had told me about and get lunch in the pub that Bill had mentioned. It would be good to meet up with him. I might find out something. My inquisitive mind has served me well in the past, and I'd always been able to sense when something was not as it should be.

On my way out, I stopped at reception to extend my stay to the weekend, which was no problem. I then made way to my car and headed towards the small town that Bill had told me about. Forty-five minutes later, I was there.

It was a small town called Somerton. It had one main street and a few small side streets. The pub, Bill had told me, was on the main street and was called "The Golden Goose". It had a car park at the rear. I was a little early for lunch, so I left the car in the pub car park and had a walk up the main street, looking at the shops and cafés, complete with outside chairs and tables. There were plenty of seaside souvenir shops.

Somerton had a small seafront. There were steps down to a shingle beach and a small wooden jetty jutting out over the sea for boats to anchor. On either side of the small beach, were cliffs, some parts eroding as the sea began to reclaim them. There were also a few beach huts for hire so that visitors could change into their beach gear. It appeared to be a normal, happy, easy-going seaside town.

Soon, it was lunchtime and time to walk slowly back to the pub.

As I walked through the pub door, I spotted Bill sitting on his own at a table. He was reading a newspaper. I sauntered over and asked him if he minded if I joined him.

He broke into a smile, stood up, shook hands and said "Of course not, it's great to see you! Sit down! Did you have any trouble finding it?"

"No, I found this place easily, and I've had a good walk around." I replied.

He explained that he was just about to order the food, and

at that very moment, a young lady wearing a pinafore came up and asked us for our order. Bill ordered a steak pie and chips, and I ordered a couple of ham toasted sandwiches. We talked about the area, and I explained that it was a few years since I had last visited. Then there was a lull in the conversation, the perfect moment for me to satisfy my curiosity.

"Did you come in your Jag today and did your driver bring you?"

I'd caught him off guard, but he explained that he had two men who accompanied him places: a chauffeur and a "go-for" to do chores. Today, they had dropped him off and taken the car back to the beach car park. He could call them when he needed picking up.

From this, I concluded that the men were, in fact, bodyguards and that they were keeping an eye on Jill. Strange.

"Does Jill have employees to drive her and do her chores too?", I asked.

He frowned. "Yes, she uses a chauffeur to drive her around."

I nodded as if it was perfectly normal.

The conversation then turned to the World Cup and athletics.

After finishing my sandwiches and downing my half-pint of lager, I stood to make my farewell. Bill was very magnanimous and asked if I'd like to go to his house for a meal that evening. I had no other plans and was delighted to accept. He drew a map on a piece of paper, and we agreed that I'd be there for 7 pm. I exited by the rear door into the car park and off I went back to the hotel.

Again, my curiosity got the better of me, and, after I had parked, I walked down the path to the beach. I stood just behind a bush to observe the beach and spotted Jill on a sun-bed under an umbrella with the two black 'suits' not far away. I went up to my room, feeling puzzled. My lunch with Bill today had made me even more sure that he was hiding something. But I did enjoy their company. I sat on my balcony with a soft drink, taking in the sun and trying to make sense of what I knew.

On the surface, Bill seemed to be a reasonable man, but it did seem to be out of character for him to live where he did. He gave the impression of enjoying luxury and being waited on, and I thought that town or city life would suit him far better. His wife was just living a life of luxury and did not seem to go anywhere without the two bodyguards by her side. Yet they had allowed me to walk with Jill for about half an hour alone last night. It seemed very odd. I was enjoying the situation, but was intrigued.

I was still pondering it when my mobile rang. It was my PA. She said that she had tried everything she could think of, but had got nowhere with finding information on the Stevens. She couldn't even find the building business owned by them. She added that there was no record on the local census of a Stevens owning any property in this area. I thanked her. How on earth could someone not have any background? It was as though they didn't exist. All I could think was that they were trying to hide from something or someone. I would have to do some more questioning.

I had time before driving to the Stevens' home to ring a friend of mine who used to be in the police, and who was now connected to MI5, the British security service. He listened carefully and then assured me that he would see what he could find out about the Stevens. "Are you enjoying yourself?" he asked.

We were old buddies, having met when we were both in the forces. I trusted him with my life.

I knew what he was getting at. "I know what you're really asking, and, yes, she is gorgeous!"

We both laughed and then said goodbye.

I just had time to shower and get ready for dinner at "Cliff House".

I drove following Bill's map and instructions, which I needed as the turning to their house was not easy to recognise. I had to turn down a narrow road, and then I came to a drive with metal gates. There was an intercom system to announce who you were. Another security measure, I guessed. As I got closer to the house, the gravel drive ended in a banjo with a statue of a cherub on the island in the middle. There was an area just off the drive where visitors could park. The black Jag was parked there. I parked there as well, and then walked up to the wide, sturdy, oak door. I rang the doorbell and waited. As I waited, my eyes surveyed the area. It reeked of affluence and privacy. I heard the door opening, and I recognised one of the 'suits', although he was now dressed as a butler.

"Good evening, sir, please follow me," he said and turned around, slowly walking towards a door at the end of the hall.

I followed him.

He opened the door and beckoned me to go in. It was a large library, full of many types of books and furnished with an oak desk and chair in the middle of the room, and a couple of large leather easy chairs nearby. On the desk was a telephone, and there was a blotting paper pad next to it. Someone must still like to use an old-fashioned fountain pen, I thought.

I sat down in one of the easy chairs and waited. Within five minutes, the door opened, and Jill came in looking as fresh and lovely as ever, maybe even a little more tanned, She smiled and looked at me. Her shoulder-length blond hair was loose, her deep blue eyes sparkled, and her off-the-shoulder white dress showed off her tanned shoulders. "I'm so glad you could come, it is lovely to meet you again. Would you like a drink?"

"No, thank you, I'm driving so I'll stick with a small wine during dinner," I replied.

She nodded. "Did you enjoy your trip to town? Bill said you went to the pub he frequents and had lunch together."

"Yes, I did," I said, "it seemed a nice place, and the food was good. Of course, that was when he invited me here to dinner."

"Unfortunately," Jill said, "he rang just before you arrived to say that he is in a meeting and will be late arriving. He wants us to start without him."

I thought it was strange, but what could I do except carry on and enjoy myself?

The table was a large one, so we sat at one end facing each

other. The butler served soup as a starter, and as we ate, I tried to guide the conversation to find out more about Jill: "Did you go to town or do anything today?"

"No, I did one or two things here and then spent time sunbathing on the beach as I like the sound of the waves in the background," she said.

"Do you visit any larger places at all?" I asked.

"Oh yes," she replied, "I go down to London once a month to see the people who deal with my business and to get financial advice."

"By train or car?" I asked.

"It depends if Bill is going. If he isn't, I travel by train."

I changed the subject: "Have you and Bill always lived in Norfolk?"

"No, we met in London at a reception he was giving for his firm. He lived there."

"Oh," I said, "what's the name of Bill's firm?"

"It's part of Stevens Holdings," she replied.

I thought it strange that my PA hadn't found this name.

We finished the soup and were served steak with all the trimmings. It was well-done, just how I liked it.

Jill turned the conversation to me, asking about my firm and whether I had to do a lot of travelling. I gave her a run down of some of the consultancy I did and explained that travel depended on where our clients were based.

"I notice you're always accompanied by the two gentlemen in black suits. Are they bodyguards or servants?" I asked.

She was quite slow in replying, "Well, I suppose a bit of both."

"Do you need a bodyguard?" I asked.

Jill became rather guarded, "Bill seems to thinks so." She looked uncomfortable, "Do you mind if we change the subject?"

"Of course not," I said.

We had just about finished the main course when the door opened, and Bill walked in. "I'm so sorry I'm late, but the meeting went on a bit, and they had arranged to have a meal brought in as well. I had no idea that they were doing that or I would not have arranged company tonight. It took so much time." He turned to Jill, "I suppose you'll want to go for your evening walk, so perhaps Ray could escort you on it while I go and get changed." He left the room, not waiting for her answer.

I told Jill that I was happy to accompany her on her walk and she nodded her agreement.

"Do you want some dessert or coffee first?" she asked.

"No, I'm fine, thank you."

"Then I'll just go and get my shawl." She informed the butler that we had finished our meal, and he escorted me back to the library while Jill went in search of her shawl.

Jill returned within a few minutes. We went out of the front door and turned right, into the garden area set out with paths, shrubs and grass. The paths were lit. We took a shrub-lined path that ran parallel to the main cliff top path.

Jill was first to speak, "I hope you enjoyed your meal."

"Yes, thank you, it was very nice, and the steak was well-done, just how I like it. The red wine was lovely too."

"Yes, it went down well," Jill murmured. She seemed guarded once more, perhaps worrying what I would ask.

To put her at ease, I complimented her on her outfit, adding how pretty she looked in it. She stopped, faced me, and gave me one of her special smiles, "Thank you for saying that," she said.

"My pleasure."

We walked a little further, then she stopped, and we both stood looking out to sea. I could just make out a yacht at anchor. She turned and looked at me. I looked into her eyes, and we kissed. Then, she put her arm in mine, and we walked on.

I felt weak at the knees and confused. The kiss had been purposeful, it had been meant to be, but Jill was a married woman.

We carried on walking, not talking, just each in our own worlds.

After a few minutes, I turned to Jill, "I don't want to put you or Bill in any position on this, but thank you for the kiss."

She stopped, gave me a peck on the cheek and said, "No problem," and carried on walking.

Soon, we were back at the front door. I wiped my face and lips and went in. I was shown to another room where Bill, dressed in less formal attire now and watching TV, was waiting. Jill left us, saying that she wanted to get into something more comfortable.

As I sat down, Bill stood up, turned the TV off, and asked if I'd like a drink. I asked for a glass of wine. Then, he asked if I'd enjoyed the walk. I nodded, commenting that I'd enjoyed looking out to sea.

"I have a yacht moored nearby," Bill said, "I've promised Jill a sail tomorrow if you'd like to join us. Have you sailed before?"

"No, not in a yacht, and I'd love to come, thank you," I replied.

Jill came in. She was dressed in a robe and still looked great.

The three of us had a drink and made small talk. Eventually, I said I would ring for a taxi to take me back to the hotel. Bill immediately offered me the services of his chauffeur. Jill accompanied me to the door, said goodnight and gave me that smile once more, followed by a peck on the cheek that sent my blood pressure soaring. I walked to the Jag and got in.

On the way back to the hotel, I pondered on how strange things were getting and started thinking about the excursion to which I had agreed. I had never sailed before. Bill had said that his yacht was an Oyster 61 deck saloon, which meant nothing to me. I would no doubt find out more tomorrow – another day and another adventure.

When I got back to my room, I took a bottle of water from the mini bar and sat on the balcony, everything going around in my head, but deep down enjoying my thoughts.

CHAPTER 3

The day out

I had been instructed to meet Bill and Jill on the beach that the hotel used. I dressed in a long-sleeve shirt, with the sleeves rolled up casually, chinos and trainers, and grabbed my sunglasses, along with a spare pair, and a small bag.

After an early breakfast, I walked out onto the beach. Jill waved to me from a small boat pulled up just onto the beach with an outboard motor on. When I got to them, one of the 'suits' and Bill pushed the boat into the sea. I climbed in, hoping I would be OK and get my sea legs quickly. It took a few minutes to get to the yacht, which, close up, looked very big. Good, I thought, at least it's not a tiny one.

Bill had two other men helping him sail it, and he soon got the sail up and started towards the open sea. There was a reasonable breeze and the canvas soon accepted it. We were off!

Jill sat on a seat near the wheelhouse and invited me to join her. "We're just going a bit further down the coast, near Yarmouth, not on a long trip. We'll be there in under an hour," she said, "Bill has some business nearby."

"Do you ever use the yacht to go abroad?" I asked.

"No, we never go abroad." Her face was serious.

This killed the conversation momentarily, so I tried again, asking if she enjoyed being on the yacht.

"Only for a short time now and then. I'm not a keen sailor," she said.

The sun was shining, and I got cooled by the occasional spray. It was a pleasant sail. We came to rest in a small bay near the cliffs, and I was told that we would take the boat with the outboard motor to the shore. On the way, Bill had been telling me how good his yacht was, being equipped with modern radio and radar, and how it was ocean-going. He added that he often went to France in it. Interesting, I thought, not with Jill then.

We disembarked into the small boat with the outboard motor, and made our way to shore, pulling the boat's bow up on the sand near the cliffs. Bill, Jill, one of the 'suits' and I got out and scrambled over the sand to the road. To my surprise, along the road was the Jag waiting to transport us to wherever they had planned. We got in and the driver set off. We passed through what I had always termed a caravan and chalet area with a few shops, in a town called Easton, and then stopped, After arranging a suitable time to pick us up, Bill and the driver dropped Jill and I off on the side of the road.

"I know a nice coffee place along this road," Jill said, "shall we go there for a start?"

"OK, lead on, I'm easy with that" I said, so we walked there and went in. It wasn't too full, and we found a seat near the window, looking out on the road and cliff top. Jill strangely seemed more relaxed when she was away from the 'suits' and Bill.

We laughed at several couples walking along the road with their children, all excited and trying to run in front, and squabbling together. I remembered those days with my children, at the age of 2-5, an enjoyable age. The families disappeared down a slope near the post office on the corner.

I mentioned this post office and slope to Jill, who said, "We could go down the slope after we finish our coffee. It leads to a nice beach in between two caravan sites."

"I'd like that," I said, and Jill seemed to get very excited and squeezed my hand. I then asked if she came here often.

She answered with a smile and said, "Once a fortnight,

when Bill has a meeting."

"Why don't you go with him?" I asked, "Don't you like the meetings, or aren't you allowed to be present?"

No smile this time, "I don't know his business, and it would bore me."

Time to change tactics, I thought. "Well, let's see what the beach brings then," and I gave a smile, which seemed to cheer her up. She started talking about how she enjoyed time on her own. We drank our coffee, then left the coffee shop, walked across the road and down the slope.

The slope looked like it served as the fishermen's boats' way to the sea. One was near the bottom of the slope with an old tractor near by. The beach was of clean sand, and there were several families with children playing, some even braving a swim in the sea.

Nearby, we found a spot that suited us, just far enough from the other sun worshippers to give us some privacy. I fetched two deck chairs, and Jill opened her bag, removing a towel and sun hat. She lay the towel on the sand before taking off her skirt and blouse to reveal a bikini. She put the hat on. My eyes were drawn to her body, but I tried not to be too obvious! I had brought a small shoulder bag, out of which I got my sun hat and put it on; I was already wearing my sunglasses. I had put on sun cream back in my room and assumed that Jill would have put some on too.

"This reminds me of my younger days on family holidays," I said.

"I hope you don't mind being here with me, it's so nice to have company for a change when I come here," Jill said.

"Well, as long as we don't stay in the sun too long," I said. "By the way, shall I go and get us some bottled water?"

"That's a good idea," she said.

I got up, "I won't be long, it's just up the slope to the post office," and off I set thinking that I would try more questions when I got back.

Within 10 minutes or so, I was heading back down the

slope with two bottles of mineral water. I couldn't see Jill at first, as she had moved nearer the cliff for shade. As I walked up, I noticed that she had got dressed and was sitting on the deck chair, rather than lying on the towel. I sat down on the other deck chair. I could see that she was shivering and looked cold.

"Is there something wrong?" I asked.

"We need to go," she said.

"Are you OK?"

"Please, just let us go," she whimpered.

I dropped the deck chairs off as we left the beach and went back up the slope. Lo and behold, at the top of the slope, was the Jag waiting for us. The chauffeur had the engine running. Jill must have used her mobile to get him here so quickly, I guessed. We got in, and I just sat quietly with my thoughts on the journey. Jill asked the driver to drop us at a pub she knew called The Red Lion.

The pub had a medium-sized saloon set out with tables for dining and a wall-mounted TV showing the football. By their welcome, it was obvious that the bar staff knew Jill well. We sat down at a table for two near a window. Jill looked at me, and no doubt my face must have shown my confusion and irritation.

"Would you like a drink?" Jill asked.

"A gin and tonic, please," I said, and she got up and went to the bar tight-lipped and pale. Time for answers, I thought.

Jill returned with two gin and tonics. I thanked her, but before I could say anything further, she looked at me and said, "Please do not ask me who made me leave the beach so fast as I cannot say."

I just looked at her for a few seconds before I replied, "Jill, you have what I consider two bodyguards and you do not have them for any reason I can think of, so, for my sake, I should be made aware of any danger or anything untoward that may or may not happen while I am with you. It's only fair."

"I take your point," she replied, "but if I tell you anything, I will have to check with Bill first, that's our agreement."

That took me aback as in my mind it pointed to him being

the problem.

She sipped her gin and tonic before continuing, "I do not want to lie to you, honestly."

I believed she meant it. I took her hand; it was cold. Something had really shaken her. "How do you feel now?" I asked.

She smiled, "Better in your company."

Hell, this was getting worse and more complicated. I mustn't let attraction colour my common sense, I thought. I couldn't believe that the first woman I'd been attracted to in years was not only married, but also had some unknown problem. Great!

After her gin and tonic, Jill began to look like her normal self again, so I suggested that we should order a sandwich.

"Yes, that would be nice," she said.

We checked the menus on the table, and then both agreed on a toasted ham sandwich. Before I went to the bar to order the food, I asked if she wanted another drink. She nodded. I ordered the food and carried our drinks back to the table. I asked her if she came here often and she replied that she came mainly in winter, when Bill was at meetings.

"Jill," I said, "I do think you should give me some idea what your problem is, but I will leave it to you to come back to me on this." I then changed the subject, and we talked a bit about the area

By the time we had finished our toasties, it was 3 pm and about time to get back to the beach and the yacht. Again, when we came out of the pub, the Jag was ready and waiting. We got in, and Jill ordered the chauffeur to take us directly back to her house. I guessed that she had gone off the idea of going back to the beach after whatever had happened there. She checked that I was OK with that.

"Yes, that will give me chance to pick up my car. I need it as I want to drive along the coast and find somewhere to eat tonight."

Jill asked me for my mobile number, and I gave it to her.

We arrived at her home at about 4 pm. She said goodbye and gave me a peck on the cheek. I got in my car and drove back to the hotel. When I got back to my room, I lay on the bed thinking. I was puzzled. Jill was an enigma. Who had frightened her so much? How could they do that without approaching her? Also, why did she have to ask Bill's permission before explaining it all to me?

I rang reception and asked if I could extend my stay to the Sunday of the following week. The receptionist changed my booking. I thanked her and put the phone down.

Then, I rang my PA and asked whether she had found out anything further. She hadn't. I rang my ex MI5 friend, but got no answer. So none the wiser still! I phoned reception again to ask if they could recommend a good restaurant not too far away and that maybe had some kind of entertainment. The receptionist recommended one about a mile down the road, a hotel called The Swan which had a female singer performing that evening. I asked the receptionist to book a taxi for 6.30 and a table for 6.45. I had an hour to wait, so I went out for a walk down to the beach.

The beach was empty, and the boat with the outboard motor was on the beach, so it was clear that Bill had returned. It seemed strange not to see Jill and the two bodyguards there. I walked down to where the sea was lapping the shore and stood looking out to sea. Suddenly, I felt as though someone was watching me. I turned around quickly. There was no-one on the beach, so I looked up to the cliff-top road. Jill stood there, but when I spotted her, she turned to walk away. Then, she turned back and gave me a wave. I raised my hand, but she had gone. I slowly made my way back to the hotel.

I showered and put on a suit, ready to go out. Then, I went down to reception to wait for the taxi. As I passed the bar, I thought I saw one of the 'suits' in there, but when I looked again, he had gone.

The taxi arrived on time, in fact, a little early, and took me to The Swan in less than ten minutes. It looked like a nice place.

I went into the lounge area, ordered wine and sat and waited for the start of the meals at 7 pm. I walked in dead on time, and a waiter escorted me to my reserved table. It was near a window and gave me a view of the garden area, with its umbrellas, tables and chairs on the lawn.

People started to come in, and I looked up at a man I thought I recognised. He turned around and came over to me. He asked if I was alone and whether I'd mind if he joined me. I recognised him as a client I had done work for and who did work in this area. He explained that he was staying overnight after having visited a client nearby. I shook hands with Derek, or Dec as he liked to be called, and assured him that he was very welcome to join me.

We started to talk a little about our business, but soon the conversation turned to football, films, shows and the heat. We had ordered a bottle of wine and soup to be followed by the main course of scampi, chips and peas. Time went quickly, and suddenly the singer came on. She was attractive, and her songs were a mixture of old classics and up-to-date ones, and she sang them all very well. She knew how to play to the audience, and most seemed to enjoy it. At the end, everyone clapped and asked for more.

During the interlude, Dec and I started talking about the local area. It turned out that he was a regular visitor and had quite a knowledge of things locally. I asked him if he knew the Whitehouse Hotel and its locality. He said that he had some knowledge and also knew people who lived nearby. I mentioned the couple I had met and their house on the cliff, which he said used to be called Cliff House. He thought they'd bought it about two years ago, and he knew that they were man, wife and staff. I commented that Bill seemed to be rather well off, and Dec replied that he was not sure, but he would see what he could find out and give me a bell. I thanked him and bought him another drink.

The singer came on stage again and Dec and I enjoyed our wine. At about 11 o'clock, I called a taxi, which arrived within

10 minutes, being local. It took me back to the hotel. I paid the taxi and walked into reception. The receptionist noticed me and called me over.

"I have a note for you, sir," she explained.

I took it and thanked her.

On arriving in my room, I opened the note. It was from Bill, asking me to see him, if I could, the next day, for lunch at the same pub as last time. OK, I thought, but I want some answers. There has to be a reason why they are so worried about being spotted and have protection.

I checked my mobile – no messages. I was too tired to sit outside tonight, so I retired for the night, my mind still working overtime.

CHAPTER 4

The two meetings

Again, the sun was shining early the next morning, and it was very warm and 'close', as my mother used to say. By the time I had showered and dressed in a long-sleeved shirt with the sleeves rolled up, cotton trousers and light shoes, I was more than ready for breakfast.

In the dining room, I sat at a table for two and ordered breakfast. Soon, more people came in, and it was about half-full when a lady came up to my table and asked if she could join me. She was auburn-haired, about late thirties, attractive and smartly dressed, in a grey skirt and white blouse. Her hair was pinned up, and there was a wry smile on her bright red lips. I told her that I'd be glad of the company, so she sat down opposite me and introduced herself as "Sue Moore, with an E".

"I'm Marriot... Ray Marriot," I said, and we shook hands. Her grip was a strong one, and I noticed that she wasn't wearing a wedding band

Like me, she ordered an English breakfast. "Have you been staying here very long?" she asked.

"No," I said, "only a few days."

"Oh, how long are you here for then?" she enquired.

"A week, maybe a fortnight, it depends how I feel at the end of this week. How about you?" I asked.

"I'm just here on a visit for a day or two," she replied.

"I see. I hope you enjoy the area. The beach is nice," I ventured to say. Then, I asked what type of job she had, and she told me that she was a 'civil servant', but avoided going into any more detail. She asked me about my work, and I told her about my consultancy.

Breakfast came, causing a lull in the conversation while we ate. When she had finished eating, she asked if I was in for dinner. I told her that I hadn't decided yet. She got up abruptly, told me that she'd probably see me again soon, and then rushed off. I sat there, puzzled. I seemed to be a magnet for unusual women. There was certainly something strange about this one as well! I got up and went back to my room.

I rang my PA for a report on the business and to see if there were any problems, and she assured me that there was nothing that she and Joan could not deal handle. I took the hint and let her get back to work. I walked out on my balcony, which gave me a view of most of the beach. I'd got my binoculars out of my car yesterday, and so I used them now, focusing them on the beach area. I could see two figures gesticulating and obviously debating something that had, by the look of it, got very heated. One was Jill, and the other was Sue, the woman who had just joined me at breakfast. The 'suits' stood quite away from them, but were keeping an eye on the exchange. Jill started to walk away, but then turned and walked back, shaking her finger at Sue. Then she turned away again and this time, did not go back, but virtually ran up the steps away from the beach.

Sue then turned to the bodyguards and started to shake a finger at them. Then, she turned and walked away towards the slope to the hotel. The two men stood talking together. Now then, I thought, what that was all that about? This must be something to do with the person or persons who frightened Jill yesterday, I thought. Sue must surely be more than a civil servant, and the black suits more than bodyguards. Why does Jill need them? I asked myself. Well, I intend to find out. They had involved me in the situation, and I could be in danger, I had a right to know. Bill, I thought, I want some answers. I concluded that they must be under some kind of government protection, but why?

By now, it was time to go along the road to the Golden Goose at Somerton to meet Bill, as his note had suggested.

I set off in my Grey Hyundai i30 at an easy speed that I felt comfortable with. After 20 minutes, I was certain that I was being followed, so I turned off the road and into the car park of a small supermarket. I parked, sat, and watched the cars coming in. The black Ford Focus that I had identified as following me turned in and parked up near the entrance. The two men in it had not seen my car, so when they went into the shop's main doors, I started up and set off once again. Five minutes later, I saw the Focus overtaking cars to try and catch up with me and keep me in sight. I put my foot down, got to Somerton and turned into a car tyre supplier before they turned the corner. Their car drove straight by. I drove out of the tyre place and turned the next corner into the Golden Goose car park. I was careful to park at the rear, where my car was not visible from the road.

I sat for a few minutes. Nobody else came into the car park, so I concluded that I had got rid of the one tailing me for the moment. I opened the car door, checked again, and then went in the rear door of the pub.

Bill was at a table for two, reading a letter by the look of it. He noticed me, and I walked over, shook hands with him and asked him what his 'tipple' was. He ordered a G & T, so I went to the bar and ordered two. While I waited, I helped myself to two menus. I took the drinks and menus over to our table, and we sat reading the menus.

"We have to talk," he said casually.

"Yes, I have come expecting to do so," I replied.

Bill, his hands making fists at his sides, slowly spoke about Jill's experience of seeing someone yesterday, someone she thought she would never see again in her life. He continued, "I can give you that information, but no more."

"It's not enough," I said, "I need to know more because what if I'm with her when this happens again, or what if we get into danger?"

He grimaced, "I cannot say more as it would put both you and us in danger if I did."

"Maybe so, but I met a lady in the restaurant this morning who had a few questions about me and then I was followed on the way here, but I gave them the slip."

He looked at me, "It looks like some things are happening that Jill and I have no control over and that your association with us has now put them onto you as a contact."

I was getting a little annoyed by the brick wall that he had put up.

"So I am involved because whoever followed me knew who I was and, as you say, has noticed my connection to you and Jill. I do not understand why my knowing you has caused this to happen. But I do know that your black-suited employees are some kind of bodyguard. I do not know if on my way home I could be stopped and accosted, do I? I cannot just accept what you have said. I may now be a "contact", but I have no clue as to what is going on!"

Bill looked very worried and assured me that he would contact someone to see what he should do. He apologised for causing me problems.

We both ordered cheese sandwiches from the young lady who came to our table. When she had gone, Bill said, "This has never happened before."

"I guess it's because Jill has been recognised now," I said, "Look, someone frightened Jill yesterday, but I'm not in a position to know whether they know where you live. My acquaintance with you two cannot have caused them to think I know either, as I was not there when Jill saw them. But how did this lady, Sue, know that I have been mixing in your company? And then there's the two that were following me today in the car. There seem to be a few involved."

Bill looked at me, "Yes, it does seem quick to have others

following you. All I can do is contact someone and see what can be done."

The sandwiches came and were quickly eaten.

"I think I will dine in the hotel this evening to see what happens." I said.

Bill excused himself, saying that he would make that phone call now to see what to do about me being followed. He didn't wait for my reply, and walked out of the room with his mobile to his ear.

He came back in about 5 minutes and sat down. He smiled. "Good news, it is the people who I deal with who were following you, just to make sure that no one else was following you."

"Great," I replied, "how long will this go on for?"

"Well, I guess it was just a one-off."

"At least that's one problem solved," I said. "I'm going to go now. I think I need some fresh air."

I left the pub by the rear door onto the car park. I checked that no one was about watching me before I set off back to the hotel. The journey back was uneventful, but I kept checking that I was not being followed. I was about halfway back when I received a call on my hands-free from my ex-MI5 friend, Mike. He asked if I was having a good holiday and told me that he was on the way to see me. I gave him directions to the hotel, and he told me that he would be spending a few days in the area so thought he would see me about his investigations. I told him that I'd book us a table for 7 pm that night, which I did when I got back to the hotel. I then went to my room and sat outside on the balcony, thinking.

After a few minutes, I took out my binoculars and looked through them. I could see Jill on a sun-bed reading and, of course, one of the black suits a few metres away. I put the binoculars down and sat contemplating things ... I must have fallen asleep, for I awoke to my room phone ringing.

"Hello, sir," said the female voice, "this is reception, Mr Marriot. We have a gentleman here asking to see you. His name is Mike...."

"Mike Sharp? Yes, I'm expecting him," I replied, "Send him up, please."

I'd just had time to splash cold water on my face, when there was a knock on the door. I opened it and greeted Mike. We shook hands, and I invited him to sit outside on the balcony. He was in his shirt-sleeves, and put his coat on a chair inside the room, walked out on the balcony and sat down. I asked if he wanted a drink and he replied that water would be good. I got him a bottle from the mini bar. He explained that he had booked into the hotel for the night, but had to leave tomorrow for a business meeting. He asked if I had anything more on the query I had given him, so I gave him a run-down on all that had happened in the last two days. He let me talk without interruption until I had finished.

He took a sip of water and said, "I am not surprised. To be honest, I keep hitting brick walls myself on any information about the Stevens. It's as though they do not exist. And with what you have just said, it does seem to point towards them being under some kind of official protection."

"Yes," I said, "I was beginning to think like that as well."

"If we are right, there is no way we can find out even their name and residence, as they will be under government protection whatever happens," he said.

"Yes, I suppose it also depends on what or who they are being protected from, and by which department." I thought of the two Russians who been poisoned just a short while ago in Wiltshire.

"The fact that they have a bodyguard is proof that their past, if they get recognised, could put them in danger," he said, "I'm afraid one of the things that they cannot protect them from is if someone from their past recognises them in their new identity, and perhaps that's what happened on the beach."

I needed to break the tension. "Well, that's another fine mess you got me into, Stanley," I said, mimicking Oliver Hardy.

We both laughed.

"Well," I said, "the only time in many years that I get the

come-on from a beautiful woman and I get all these problems too! But, to be honest, they have been very decent company."

Mike said that all I could do was to give it a bit longer and see what happened.

"Maybe you are right," I agreed.

He stood up, "I will just go back to my room and have a shower before we eat, so I'll meet you in the bar near the restaurant." He picked his coat up and left.

I too had a shower and got changed. This could be an interesting evening, I thought as I went down to the bar near the dining room. I had just sat down in the bar area when Mike walked in. We ordered a bottle of wine, and then we were shown through into the restaurant, to a table for four near the window. We both picked up menus and studied them.

Slowly, the room started to fill, and our bottle of Pinot Grigio was brought to us in an ice bucket. I poured a glass out for each of us. We both tasted it and agreed that it hit the spot.

A waitress asked if we would like to order. We both ordered soup starters, and I asked for gammon, chips and peas, as I like to indulge in what I call 'pub grub' when I can, and Mike ordered scampi, chips and peas, as he was very much like me on food preferences.

As I sipped my wine, my eyes scanned the room. I couldn't see anyone I knew, but then, suddenly, a woman's voice asked: "Can I join you, gentlemen?"

I turned around. It was Sue Moore.

"Yes, of course, it's been a long time since I last spoke to you," Mike said.

I just sat with my mouth open. So, he knows her, I thought.

"When Ray said that a lady had sat with him at breakfast called Sue Moore, I didn't recognise the name, but I never forget a face, do I?" Mike said to her.

"Well, you wouldn't know my married name, would you?"

Mike nodded, "Has it been that long?"

And they both smiled.

I offered her a glass of wine, and she accepted. I beckoned

the waiter over and asked if Sue wanted to order, telling her what
we had ordered. She ordered soup to start, followed by steak with
all the trimmings.

Mike controlled the conversation, asking her about her
marriage, whether she was divorced now, and then touching
on whether she was still with the 'department'. She smiled, and
Mike nodded his head. Sue asked me how I knew Mike, and I
told her of our time together in the forces, after which he had
joined MI5:

"We served two years in the Royal Marines Commandos
and were both lieutenants. We've seen and experienced many
things you never discuss, and served on many things together.
We became friends forever, both having saved each other's lives in
the process. We learnt how to kill in many, many different ways
and during our term had to see and experience many things you
have to forget and put out of your mind, and we were good at
it. I took my demob and finished. Mike kept on and eventually
ended up in MI5 for many years, but eventually, he finished
and became a private investigator, and, to this day, he still is." I
explained.

Sue sat quietly while I said all this, then turned to Mike and
asked how he had got out of MI5. He smiled and said that it was
a case of it's not what you know, but who you know, and winked.

"You don't change, do you?" She said, and watching her
face, I got the feeling that they had been more than friends at
one time.

Our soup came all together, even though Sue had ordered
after us. Sue began to speak again, "Ray, I'm sorry you are
involved in this, and it is very unfortunate that you, or rather
Jill, came across someone she never expected to ever see again at
the beach It may be a one-off, and nothing will come of it, or,
if it is not a one-off, then we will soon find out. I can't say more
than that."

"Well," I said "thank you, at least for that, but I will never
know if I am being followed and who they are. I also do not like
anyone to be bullied or controlled without their acceptance, or

for their free rights to be abused. I will give it some time and still see Bill and Jill. Also, I have to admit that I have feelings for Jill."

Sue looked at me with a knowing look on her face, "I could tell, and she certainly has for you. Part of my job,", she continued, "is being able to assess people, and I assess you as a genuine person with the right intentions, and I know Mike, and if he says you're OK, then you are!"

We finished our soup, and the main course appeared. We were all hungry and soon got stuck into demolishing them. We then started to talk about trivia: from TV to football, to the Olympics, the armed forces, and so on. We finished the main course, and like Mike and me, Sue did not want a sweet or a coffee. She stood up, "It was nice to see you again, Mike, and, Ray, take care."

She left very quickly, and Mike and I just looked at each other for a few seconds, before he spoke, "I think it's what we thought, protection.. MI5".

"Yep," I said, "give it time, but stay aware. I have only just over a week before I go home, should be long enough."

Mike said that he had a few calls to make and he felt tired, so he was turning in for the night. I said that I wanted to go for a walk before I turned in. We both stood up and went our separate ways. I walked by the reception and out of the front door and down to the beach. It was dusk. I sat on a sun bed and looked out to sea. My phone rang. I didn't recognise the number, but answered it. The voice that replied to my "Hello" was Jill's.

"Ray, I hope you do not mind me ringing you, but I judged that you would have finished your meal by this time, so I thought I would try now. Are you OK?"

"Yes," I said, "and perhaps I understand a little bit more now."

"Oh," she replied, "I'm glad, as I hoped it would not stop our friendship continuing."

"Well, it has altered the fact of perhaps thinking more where we go, but nothing else," I replied.

"I am so glad. Would you like to go for a trip along the

coast with us tomorrow? If you come to our house and park, we will have the chauffeur drive us about."

"Sounds good to me, about what time?" I asked.

"Would 10 am be OK?" she said.

"Fine," I remarked, and she hung up.

I returned to my hotel room,got into bed and went to sleep exhausted.

CHAPTER 5

Another day out

When I awoke, I felt rather hungover. Had I drunk that much? Perhaps it was a combination of alcohol and tiredness.

Sunlight was already filling the room, so I got out of bed and showered, which helped to bring me round. A full English breakfast with toast had me feeling back to normal by the time I had packed a few items in my shoulder bag, put it in the boot of my car and driven off, heading for Cliff House.

At the house, I collected my bag from the boot and walked up to the front door where Jill was standing talking to one of the 'suits'. As I approached, she looked up, gave me a big smile and asked the 'suit', who was obviously acting as our chauffeur, to put my bag in the boot.

She hugged me, "We're going to a private area the other side of Great Yarmouth. It belongs to a friend and has its own beach, log cabin and small woodland area. Bill is coming too, but when we get to the cabin, he has to travel on a bit to a business meeting. He'll meet up with us again this afternoon." She went on to explain that she had prepared a picnic basket for us, and I thanked her. Bill came out and shook my hand, saying that he was pleased I was joining them today.

We all got in the car, and it set off, heading inland, off the coast road, to the better and faster roads that went in the direction of Great Yarmouth. We made small talk and soon we were turning off the main road and down a narrow lane. The lane opened out into a driveway in front of a log cabin. Beside it, there were stables, fences, and logs that needed chopping for winter, and there was a veranda with a table and several chairs for al fresco eating. We went in, and Bill and Jill opened doors and windows to air the cabin. It was equipped with a generator already primed and ready to go, so we switched it on to get the fridge working for the food, wine and milk we had brought. Bill made a couple of phone calls and after a quick drink said that he had to be off. "Do you have your phone?" He asked Jill.

She nodded.

"I should be back about 3!" He called back as he got in the Jag.

Jill decided to make a cup of tea for us to have on the veranda. "We can drink our cuppa and relax while we wait for the car to come back," she explained, "then we can decide what we want to do.

She was obviously keen to have the bodyguard close at hand, I thought.

Jill brought the tea out on a tray, placed it on the veranda table, and poured us a cup each. We looked at each other, and I broke the silence, "I never thought we would be doing something like this together after your fright on the beach."

"Well, I had my doubts," she said, "but I was determined to carry on as normal, if it was possible." She smiled warmly.

"How do you feel now?" I asked.

"OK, fine in fact," she said. "I don't know if they actually spotted me, but I was so shocked to see them, I just wanted to get away."

"Maybe they didn't see you," I commented, "and, if so, there's no harm done. But at least we know that they're in the area and so can take precautions." I changed the subject then, asking if she had been to this cabin before.

"Yes, a couple of times," she answered, "it's a lovely place, and it having its own private beach as well is a real bonus."

I finished my tea and told Jill that I'd like to walk around and acquaint myself with our surroundings, but before she could reply, the Jag turned into the driveway.

"Excuse me a minute," Jill said as she walked over to the Jag. She had a short conversation with the driver, who then got out and walked into the cabin.

"I let him know that we're going for a walk along the coastal path and back. He reminded me to take my phone," she said.

Jill went and got her bag. I picked up my bag and shouted a farewell to the driver. We set off down the drive, turned right after about fifty paces and then started along a narrow path through some trees, before suddenly appearing on the cliff top path. It was a warm sunny day, and the view out to sea was breathtaking. A few yards further along the path were steps down to the beach - a bit steeper than the ones to Cliff House, but well constructed and with decent handrails to hold on to if needed.

"We could go down to the beach after lunch," said Jill, "but for now, we'll walk a bit further along the path and through the trees."

I nodded.

We stood there, just looking down at the beach and enjoying our time together. A plane flew over, going at quite a speed. We looked up.

"That's going out to sea at a fair rate, I wonder if they have been scrambled." I commented. Jill just smiled.

We walked along the path, which turned to the right, through some trees. With the singing of birds in the trees, the sound of the surf on the beach, and the humming of bees, Jill seemed at peace. Suddenly, she stopped, turned to me, came closer, and kissed me passionately. I hadn't experienced a kiss like that for many years, and I returned it. We broke apart. "It's a pity that we've met now, and you are married," I said.

Jill smiled, "It's only a little further along here." She said.

I wiped my mouth and face with a tissue I had in my pocket. We came out of the trees and bushes at the side of the log cabin and walked to the front door. The chauffeur was busy washing the car. Jill shouted to him, asking if he wanted any food, and he replied that he'd already eaten.

Jill asked me to take the picnic basket and put it on the table in the veranda, adding that it would be cooler there. She offered me wine, but I thought it would be wiser to stick to water today, and then she asked if I minded spending the afternoon on the beach, adding that there were sunbeds and umbrellas available for our use.

"Not at all," I said, "the weather's too hot to do anything too energetic," and she gave me a cheeky smile.

We cleared the table and Jill had words with the chauffeur, checked her bag, and then we set off down to the beach.

We decided to stay in the shade of the cliffs. As we lay on the sunbeds, we started with small talk that developed into me asking more questions: what did she do in the winter when she couldn't sun bathe? Did she have any hobbies? Did they go abroad for the winter?

Jill said that she didn't have any hobbies worthy of mention and that they didn't go abroad. She used the chauffeur to take her on trips in the local area.

I asked whether Bill accompanied her on any trips.

"No, not very often," she replied.

What a life and what a marriage! I thought, "Don't you go to any shows in London?" I asked.

"I have been once," she said.

I changed my questions then. "Have you any plans for the future at all?"

I could see she was getting edgy now, so I added, "OK, sorry, you don't have to answer that." But, surprisingly, she commented that it would be nice to plan for the future.

Just for a moment, we were in a world of our own, but then suddenly, above us, there was a helicopter, heading from land out to sea. "It looks like it's looking for someone," I said, "maybe someone's in trouble."

We watched it circling over the sea, near the cliff.

"Do you get many of those here?" I asked.

"No," she replied.

I was uneasy. "Just get the things together when it heads to sea again, and before it comes this way. We'll take the steps up into the trees, just in case."

The helicopter headed out to sea once more, made a big circle, and then flew out of sight. We dashed up the steps and got under cover in the trees. The helicopter came over again and then turned up the coast and away from us.

"I may be overreacting, but it's better to be safe than sorry," I said.

Jill nodded, and we walked back under the trees and headed to the cabin. There, Jill asked the driver if he had seen the helicopter. He had, and explained how he'd gone into the cabin.

"If it was who I think it was, I hope they didn't recognise the car," I ventured to say. The driver walked away, took out his mobile and made a call.

"Let's stay inside and listen out for the helicopter," I said to Jill. "But perhaps your driver could ring around and find out if the coastguard, police, or air ambulance have been out in this area. It would be good to know whether we are being over-cautious at the moment."

Jill nodded then went to speak to him again.

"I'll put the kettle on for a pot of tea, the drink that we British consider the answer to every thing! Although, I have always found it does calm you and gives you time to think." I said.

Jill was sitting on the lounge settee when I took the tray through. "I'll play mother and pour," Jill said.

"Now this is cosy and domesticated, isn't it?" I said, as Jill offered me milk and sugar.

"Does that worry you?" She asked, looking at me.

I laughed, "No, of course not."

Although I was uncomfortable feeling that I had to look over my shoulder, not knowing whether we were being watched, I really did enjoy Jill's company.

There was a knock on the door, it opened, and the driver made his way over to Jill and gave her a note to read. He left the room. Jill read the note, "Well it appears that the coastguard has used a helicopter to search for two missing lads, They've been found now, though."

"Good, that's two pieces of good news, " I said, "the boys have been found, and we over-reacted."

"Better that way than to be sorry later," she said. "I do appreciate you being patient and trusting me."

"I realise that you need to be protected, but not knowing what I am up against is difficult. For instance, can we do a trip around Norfolk or are we only to go to places like this? Places that are private? Although I don't mind the perk of having our own chauffeur!"

Jill sat in silence.

"I mean, would it be possible to visit different areas along the coast? I do enjoy your company."

Jill smiled, "I'd love to do that with you, and it would be such a change. I'll find out if I can. I really do appreciate your annoyance at not knowing what's going on, and I will ask," she assured me. She had such a look of determination on her face!

Then, her phone rang, and she excused herself, leaving the room to answer it. She soon came back, telling me that Bill had finished his meeting and had suggested that we pick him up. I agreed to the plan, and Jill told Bill that we'd set off in ten minutes. After she'd hung up, she sat next to me, took my hand in hers and gave me a peck on the cheek.

"Thank you," she said, as she looked into my eyes. Then, she broke the spell, walked to the door and shouted to the driver to let him know that we were all going to pick Bill up.

Ten minutes later, Bill was in the car with us.

"I heard that you had another problem," he said.

Neither of us replied for a moment, not knowing what to say, and then I explained, "We weren't sure if we were being over-cautious, but not knowing if Jill was compromised, being over-cautious was the only way to stay safe."

"I quite agree," he replied, "and we should know in a few days whether she is or not, I should think."

"Maybe so. The sooner the better." I said.

We continued on to Cliff House and parked.

As I got out of the car, Bill asked if I'd like to have a glass of wine with him in the library. I agreed to it, and Jill said that she was going to go for a quick shower before joining us.

I followed Bill into the library and sat in one of the easy chairs. A tray with two bottles on it, one red wine and the other white, was brought in.

"I noticed you like a Pinot Grigio," Bill said, "so I have had one chilled and brought in for you."

I smiled, and nodded my agreement.

Bill gave me a glass of the white and poured himself a glass of the red. We said 'cheers', and then both started on our wine.

Bill commented on my prudent actions regarding the helicopter episode. I expressed my concern over the situation: "How can I, or indeed you two, go anywhere at the moment, when we know that someone from Jill's past could show up at any time?"

He looked at me, "Yes, Jill really does have a problem."

"Can you expand on this?" I asked.

He looked away, "No, not really."

I considered that it was time to lay our cards on the table. "OK, is she in any danger? And how long has this been going on? Are your two bodyguards protecting just her? How can you go anywhere you want on business, but she is so limited?"

He gave me a very serious look, "I am very limited in what I can say," he explained, "but, I can say that the two helpers are mainly to protect her. I haven't got the enemies that she has. Her enemies are from another country and before this week, she thought that she'd left them behind there and that she was safe in the UK."

"I appreciate your candour," I said, "I don't like anyone, governments or organisations, ruling peoples freedom."

"If we tell you everything, we'd have to move on and start all over again." He said. He then changed the subject, "Would you like to come for dinner? I've invited another guest: Sue. I believe you've already met her."

"Yes, I'll come," I said, and then excused myself, saying that I needed to go back to the hotel to make some phone calls. I stood up, shook his hand, and asked him to explain to Jill that I had to go, but would see her that evening."

I made my way back to the hotel. I felt frustrated as I seemed to be getting nowhere with my questions. I sat in my car, thinking for a while. Then, I calmed down and concluded that they had only just met me and perhaps it was too soon for them to trust me. Plus it seemed that they weren't calling the shots anyway, there were being controlled by MI5 personnel, one of whom I would be seeing at the meal tonight. Perhaps I could quiz her.

I had time to go down to the hotel beach and have a look around the area near the far cliff that went around to the cove. Standing nearby, with his foot resting on a small boat, was a ruddy-faced man, obviously a local.

"Good afternoon," I said, "do you ever go out to the cove on the other side of this cliff?"

He smiled, "Every day," he said, "it has caves as well, but I've never bothered to explore them."

"Oh," I said, "I was just curious because some nights I see torchlight near here and wondered what is was."

He grunted, "Probably folk from the yacht anchored out at sea near the cove entrance, they use this area a lot."

"Have you never seen the lights, then?" I asked.

"Well, only once, but they soon disappeared. I will keep my eyes open now though," he said.

I thanked him before turning and walking back to the hotel.

Back in my room, I took off my shirt and took a bottle of water out onto the balcony. As I sat there, I tried to get my thoughts together on Bill and Jill's position. I thought they must be asylum seekers who had something the government wanted - enough to accept them and give them a new identity and residence. But they'd also been given bodyguards and now had been spotted by their home government, who were obviously not happy with them leaving. Which country had they left and why? And why was Jill the focus?

Patience, Ray, patience, I told myself, it will unfold soon. And I want to carry on seeing Jill, and I was sure she felt the same. I looked down at my watch. It was time to shower and get ready.

PART TWO

CHAPTER 6

More Exploring

At Cliff House, I was greeted by a butler and taken to the library where Bill and Sue were waiting. Jill soon joined us, and we headed off into the dining room, where Bill and Sue sat opposite Jill and me.

The first course was soon served, wine was poured into glasses, and the conversation began.

"Sue has been informed of everything that's taken place so far, and feels that we are doing everything right," Bill said.

"I'm sure you are, I said, "but, not knowing if there is any danger from these other people is not so good for me. I can't prepare myself for something I don't know about or understand."

"I cannot say too much, but there may well be danger for you if they have spotted Jill,"Sue said.

The main course arrived, and there was silence for a minute or two as everyone began eating.

"Can I make a suggestion? Why not hire another car so that if Jill and I want to explore while you're busy, Bill, a bodyguard can drive us and stay with us. That means that Jill is always protected."

Sue nodded, "It may well be worth considering," she said.

After the main course, we all declined dessert. Bill and Sue retired with their coffees to the library, while Jill and I decided to give coffee a miss and go for a walk.

It was dusk and there was just enough light enough to see the breakers on the shore below. We stood watching and listening to the surf. There was a heavenly scent from the flowers along the path. All our worries were forgotten for a minute.

"It's lovely having someone to walk with," Jill said, and then she kissed me. Laughing, she added, "I could get used to this."

"I'm getting used to it," I said, smiling.

"I do hope we get a chance to explore the coast together sometime," She said as we walked on.

"Yes, I hope so too," I said.

We stopped again. I put my arm around her shoulder and she leaned her head against my shoulder.

"I wish it could be like this all the time," I said, "I'd love to be able to go anywhere we want without asking permission."

Jill nodded.

"It's hard for me to know nothing and yet feel that I have to protect you. I've been thinking about it, and I've concluded that you are under the protection of MI5 and need bodyguards in case of someone from your past recognising you."

She looked up to me, "I can understand you being confused. I hate it too as I keep being told what is best for me."

She looked worried, so I quickly assured her: "I was not trying to cause problems, and I don't want to stop seeing you." I smiled. She smiled back, and gave me a peck on the cheek. Then, we stood there, our arms around each other, our eyes locked.

"Let's just enjoy what we have together," I said. We stayed like that for a few minutes before turning back to the house.

Bill and Sue were sitting talking when we entered the library. I looked at my watch and excused myself, saying that I needed an early night. They each shook hands with me in turn, and Jill showed me to the door, where she gave me a peck on the cheek. When I got to my room, I decided that my mind was buzzing too much to sleep, so I went and sat on the balcony. It was like doing a jigsaw puzzle, but the pieces didn't fit. Why was Jill the problem? Why not Bill? He was the one that seemed to have secrets. It was all such a mystery. The next morning I got up early and decided to go down for breakfast. Just as I was heading out of my door, the phone rang. It was Mike asking how things were. I brought him up-to-date and then asked him about asylum seekers, and how things worked with embassies and customs, and people entering the country. Surely embassies were aware of people coming and going, and surely MI5 or the embassy would know if Jill's enemies had entered the country and be able to warn Bill and Jill to be on their guard. Of course, they may well be using assumed names or have entered illegally. All Mike said was that he would make enquiries about the situation and get back to me, if and when he could.

Nobody joined me for breakfast, so I was alone with my thoughts. When I returned to my room, my mobile rang; it was Jill.

"What are your plans today?" she asked.

"Well, I thought I might explore further along the coast, near the cove and caves."

Jill enthusiastically asked if she could join me, adding that Sue had agreed that she could come out with me if we took a driver along with us. "But the other car doesn't arrive until later today, so could we go in your car?" she asked. I agreed and said I'd be leaving for her house in a few minutes.

Jill was at the front door waiting for me as I pulled into the driveway.

"I have asked for a picnic hamper to be made up for us and thought we could go to the cliff first," she said as I walked up to her.

"Great," I said, "I've brought my binoculars."

I followed Jill through the shrubbery and out onto the long grass on the cliff tops. We stood under a tree, and I looked at the area that had three caves, all big enough to sail a small boat into. The same yacht I'd noticed previously was anchored just off the coastline. Unfortunately, there was no activity at the yacht or near the cave. I scanned the sea and cliffs: nothing. I turned to go.

"Is that all you wanted to do? Jill asked.

"Yes, I just wanted to check."

She looked puzzled but didn't say anything. We turned around and walked back along the path to the house. As we approached, the driver came out and asked me for my car keys so that he could put the picnic hamper in the boot. Then, Jill and I got in the back, and the driver took us down the coast road. It was rather different being a passenger in my own car!

After about ten miles, I noticed an old sign for the beach. I asked the driver to turn off the road to explore what was down the road. A narrow gravel road opened out into a slightly wider road and eventually into a gravel car park. The driver parked the car and stayed with it, while Jill and I walked down a slope to a pretty little sandy beach.

"Do you want to walk along the beach or sunbathe?" I asked Jill.

Jill replied that she'd like to explore along the beach. We set off along the sand, Jill removing her shoes. We kept in the shade of the cliff, away from the young families building sandcastles. Suddenly, I heard the sound of a helicopter. Soon, it was above us, hovering. I felt Jill stiffen.

"Just act normal," I said, "and walk nearer the cliff and back up the slope. Take it slowly, don't rush, and let's see what they do. You have your wide-brimmed hat on, and that covers a lot of your face, so they can't tell who you are from above. I'll come with you and hide you from the side."

We slowly walked back towards the slope, hand-in-hand like a couple just enjoying a seaside walk. The helicopter moved out to sea to turn, and then headed further up the coast. I wished I had kept my binoculars with me so that I could have made out the markings on the helicopter and have known if it was just the coastguard or air ambulance. We came to the slope, and I looked up to see our driver standing at the top, watching us. He had obviously seen the helicopter. At least today he was wearing cotton trousers and a short-sleeve shirt and looked more like a holidaymaker.

I turned to Jill and asked if she wanted to continue our walk or drive further up the coast, adding that I didn't think that the helicopter was anything to do with us. Jill chose to go back to the car. As we drove along the coast, the driver repeated what I'd said about the helicopter, but Jill just nodded. After about 45 minutes, we came across a chalet-park in a wooded area. We turned in and drove past wooden chalets and brick ones, along the road to a few shops, before parking in the car park. We got out and walked along the path that obviously led to the beach. This beach was a lot busier, with people sunbathing and having fun in the sea. Along the path, near the cliffs, was a row of beach huts with people sitting outside them on deck chairs enjoying the sun.

We decided to walk along the beach. Jill took her shoes off once again, and we set off, Jill this time insisting that we walk along the water's edge to paddle. We could see a ship in the distance. This time, I had my binocular, so we paused and I looked at it through them – nothing unusual.

We were soon hot and tired, so we decided to go back to the car so that we could find a café for a drink and a sandwich. As we walked, I reminisced about beach holidays I'd enjoyed with my children.

Meanwhile, back at the chalet park, on a veranda outside one of the brick chalets, two well-built men sat talking.

"Ivan," said the slightly smaller of the two. He was clean-shaven and wearing a blue shirt and grey trousers. "Did you see the couple with a driver just coming from the beach?"

"Yes," replied his companion, who sported a short salt-and-pepper beard. "She looked familiar, didn't she?"

"Yes, I think so. I took a photo with my phone and I'll send it to HQ to see if they can get a match."

"Yes, you do that," said Ivan, "It's too warm to go rushing about. Alexei, let them do the work." He lit a cigar and leaned back in his chair.

Alexei stood up, walked to the edge of the veranda and looked over at the car park. He watched as a grey car passed, drove to the car park exit, and turned left on the coast road. He shouted to Ivan: "They've just left!"

He had just said this when his phone rang. Alexei sat down with the phone to his ear. "I'm at the chalet park, why?" He asked, then: "Who did you say you think it is?... Yes, we will get straight off and see if we can catch up with them."

He turned to Ivan, "They're sending an email with a blown-up picture of the woman on it. We need to catch them up and verify if it is the blond woman who's supposed to be dead."

"Let's go! We can check the email on our mobiles." Ivan replied, and the two men rushed out to their card and sped off. Our driver parked my car in the shade of some trees in the little car park of a café I knew from past visits to the area. "I'm not coming in, I have some water here," said the driver, "and I have some calls to make."

We went inside the café, which was similar to the roadside restaurants that used to be dotted around the UK. I ordered toast and tea for two.

"I'm really enjoying this ride out and the places we have been to so far," said Jill.

"Yes," I said, it's nice to explore. I'm enjoying it as well. Sorry if I overreacted about the helicopter," I added, "but it's better to be safe than sorry."

Jill frowned, but nodded.

"Well," I said, "let's enjoy our freedom while we can."

She smiled, and we sat and enjoyed our tea and toast. Jill talked a little about her childhood in Russia. Her family had started off not so well off, but by the time she was college age her father had saved up enough money to send her and her brother to a college in England, and she ended up at the University of Leicester. She told me that she had enjoyed university life and the freedom that came with it. She'd graduated with a degree in languages. When she left university, she stayed on in England for a time, and then married a man she'd met at uni, a fellow Russian and a man who had very strict communist ideals. After a few years, Jill and her and husband went back to work in Russia, and she got a good job as an interpreter, while he joined the then re-vamped KGB, which changed into the FBS, although keeping those methods favoured by the KGB. The marriage soon ended in divorce, and by this time, Jill's brother, Bill, had began making money and doing well for himself with Kremlin contracts. These were secret classified contracts, so when Bill decided to go back home to the UK, the Russians were not very happy.

"And that's where we are now," said Jill, "I came with him for a better life and freedom, and also to prevent them using me as leverage to get to him. But, if they find out I am still alive, we will be on their most-wanted list."

I looked at Jill, took her hand in mine, and said: "I won't let you come to any harm."

We had finished eating and drinking, so we headed back to the car where the driver was sitting with all the windows down. He started the car and set off on the coast road once more.

Alexei and Ivan had driven along the coast road for several miles when they realised that unless the ones they were after had been breaking the speed limit for nearly half an hour, then they must have turned off onto another road. They decided to turn round and go back to the chalet park. After about 15 minutes, they recognised the grey car heading towards them and going in the opposite direction. Alexei made a sudden u-turn. "Idiot," muttered Ivan, "now they'll know they're being followed! Don't get too near, but keep them in sight."

I'd noticed a car going in the other direction do a sudden u-turn. "Did you see that?" I asked our driver.

"Yes, I'm going to call it in," he said.

I turned to Jill, "Don't panic, but I think we may have company."

I heard the driver's boss tell him that they didn't have a car in the vicinity. "Then we need to lose them or make them follow us into a trap with you," I said.

The voice replied: "The nearest car we have is only a mile from Cliff House."

"OK, then we can get them to follow us to near there, and

you can be ready to apprehend them."

The driver hung up.

"You're coming up to two slow bends," I said to him. "And then there's a large entrance to a factory. I want you to swing into the entrance and turn right onto the coast road. They'll turn round to follow us, and we can keep them in sight until we're near your people."

The driver turned the bend, swung into the large factory entrance, and turned the car ready to go right onto the coast road. The car following us went by, pulled into a entrance further on and then turned to come back along the coast road.

"Well, that proves that they are definitely following us," I said, "Let's go!"

We travelled at a good pace. "I think we'll lead them a chase for a while to give your people time to get sorted out." I pointed to the next road on the left, and the driver took it.

The other car followed us down it and after a mile I told the driver to turn right at the next road, which I knew would lead us back to the coast road eventually.

He turned at the right time. They were two cars back and nearly missed it. I smiled and said to nobody in particular, "That will upset them I bet."

Alexei was very occupied with watching the grey car and hanging back the right amount, leaving four car lengths between them. Beside him, Ivan was watching as well. They slowed for a bend and then accelerated out of it, when Ivan suddenly glimpsed the grey car turning round. "They're turning back!" he shouted, "find somewhere where we can turn back quickly!"

Alexei swung the car into an entrance, and did a u-turn.

"Damn, " said Alexei, "they must have seen us!" He put his foot down, but carefully, keeping at least two cars between them.

The grey car turned right, heading off the coast road, and Alexei followed, keeping his distance. About a mile later, he glimpsed the boot of the grey car disappearing down another right-hand turn and had to brake sharply to make the turn in time. The car behind him blasted its horn.

"They're trying to lose us," Ivan said, "we can't let them!"

Jill was sitting there, ashen-faced.

"Don't worry," I reassured her, "I will make sure you're OK, I promise."

She nodded and squeezed my hand.

The driver's phone rang, and he answered it on speaker phone.

"I have just been told what is happening," Sue's voice rang out.

"Thank goodness!" I said, "I'm worried about where to stop and how to make sure they don't get away."

"We are setting up some traffic lights for roadworks," she said.

"Sounds good to me," I replied. "Will everything be in place by the time we get there?"

"Yes, they're being put in position as I speak."

"Great. I'm sure Jill will feel better when this is done with."

"Jill, take care, and trust what your driver tells you to do," Sue said, and hung up.

Our driver informed us that he was slowing down, "I can see the roadworks ahead," he added.

We approached the roadworks slowly, and the lights changed to red. Ivan and Alexei were keeping a sharp eye on the grey car ahead.

"We need to figure out how to approach them," Ivan said.

"Looks like roadworks ahead," Alexei said.

"Perhaps that will help us to get a bit closer," Ivan commented.

As they approached the traffic lights, there were three cars ahead of them: the grey car at the front, and then two cars in between. The workmen were talking to each car in turn, so Ivan lowered the window.

"Sorry to bother you, sir," said the workman, "but if you look behind you, you will see men pointing their guns at you. Please get out of the car with your hands in the air."

Ivan and Alexei did as they were told.

"Now put your hands on top of the car."

They did. They were handcuffed and transferred to another car, while another workman took possession of their car. The light changed to green and our driver went through the roadworks and pulled onto the side of the road.

"I couldn't see what happened," I said, but just as I said that, a car came and parked behind us.

Our driver got out, walked to the other car, and began a conversation with the driver.

"It looks like the roadworks idea panned out," I said, "and that the men following us were apprehended."

She smiled, held my hand and squeezed it, but said nothing.

Our driver returned to the car and informed us that two Russian agents had been apprehended. These were men that the authorities had been trying to catch for a while, he added, and a photo of Jill had been found in their car. They had been taken for questioning. Our driver also informed us that we could return to Cliff House. So we did, and as we parked, I noticed a black Range Rover parked there.

Jill invited me in for a drink, and I was shown to the room where I had left Jill and Bill the other night. The butler brought in a tray of tea, which he put on the coffee table in front of the settee where we were sitting. Jill poured us a cup each, and we both gratefully took a sip of it.

"Well," I said, "that was all a bit traumatic!"

She looked at me with a rather worried look on her face, "It proves that they are looking for me," she said, "but we should know more when Sue rings."

Realising she was worried, I said "Yes, it must be very disturbing that they are. Why now, after all the time you have been here?"

"I don't know," she replied, and then changed the subject to ask me what I was doing that evening.

"I think I will dine in my hotel," I said.

"I guess we will be seeing Sue, but if we sort things out by the time we need a meal, would you mind if we joined you?" Jill asked.

I smiled, "Of course, any time."

I told Jill that I needed to go, as there were calls that I needed to make. She gave me a peck on the cheek, and I left, heading back to the hotel.

CHAPTER 7

The aftermath of the chase

As I passed reception, the receptionist called me over, informing me that a note had been left for me. It was from Mike, asking me to ring him on my return.

In my room, I poured myself a glass of water and sat out on the balcony. There, I rang Mike on my mobile. We exchanged pleasantries, and I told him all that had happened that day. He listened patiently.

"It sounds like the net is closing in on Bill and Jill," he said, "and it seems like agents from multiple countries are after them. But it also means that they have something that we, the British want," he added, "and it worries me that Bill and Jill will end up disappearing before we can find out. How do you feel about it all, Ray?" He asked.

"Well, as you have probably guessed, I have feelings for Jill, and don't want to lose her. And I hate the idea of other countries controlling their lives; it's not right. I will help Jill in any way that I can. She told me that Bill is her brother, too, rather than her husband."

"I'll come and visit you as soon as I can," Mike replied, "and we'll see what we can make of all this." He hung up.

I rang reception and booked a table for later. Then, I just sat on my balcony thinking of all that had happened that day.

Suddenly, my mobile rang.

"Ray, is it possible for you to come here for a meal this evening, please," Jill said, "Sue and Bill both think it would be good to have your views on today as well."

"OK," I agreed, and we arranged a time. I rang reception and cancelled my reservation. Then, I used my binoculars to scan the beach.

There were still a few people on sunbeds, being served by waiters bringing them drinks. Most seemed to be couples, and then there was a lady by herself. The sea was calm, and the sun looked hot. Nothing seemed out of the ordinary or worth a second look.

I showered and got ready for the evening ahead. Then, I set off for Cliff House. After my arrival there, the butler escorted me straight to the room I called the "lounge". There, Bill and Jill were sitting on the settee, while Sue was sat in an armchair. I took the other armchair.

After greeting them all, I waited for Sue to say something, but it was Bill who spoke first, "I'm sorry about what happened this afternoon," he said, "I hope you're OK."

"Yes," I replied, "but I'm worried that I'm more involved in the situation now, because it was my car they were following, and they'll now have my registration and details."

"From our interviews with the men," Sue explained, "I think they were just errand boys sent to follow Jill and report back. I don't think they dug any deeper. Fortunately, we have one or two cases we think they were involved in, so we can hold them for a while. However, they may well be missed, and the Russians might start trying to find them."

"And what about Jill?" I asked, "Now they know she's in the area."

Sue looked at Jill, then turned to me and commented that it was a difficult situation.

"O, what a tangled web we weave when first we practise to deceive," I couldn't help muttering. The others looked at the floor. "I don't enjoy being pushed around, and I feel that I have the right to live my life without looking over my shoulder with fear, so I am certainly not quivering in my shoes. What do we do, though?" I asked.

"Well, the three of you must take precautions," Sue said.

"Such as?" I asked.

"Only use the cars provided and take a driver with you whenever you go out," she continued. "And stick to places like the log cabin, beach, the pub, Bill's work, and the hotel, and check with us if you need to go somewhere different."

I shrugged my shoulders, Jill looked a bit unsure, but Bill seemed relieved.

"OK, it's worth a try, I think," I said. The others looked relieved at my answer.

The butler came in and announced dinner was ready, so we all followed him into the dining room.

Over dinner, we made small talk for a while, and then I asked Sue whether she and headquarters were going to be doing more investigating. She nodded, "Of course, but I cannot tell you more."

We all declined dessert and Jill and I decided to take a walk. We walked along the path that joined the coastal path, and I put my arm around her shoulders and squeezed her. "Has today's débâcle shaken you and worried you?" I asked.

She stopped and looked at me. She had a worried look on her face, "Yes, I'm worried. They know I'm here now, and they'll continue to look for me until they know where I live. And I'm worried about involving you. You didn't sign up for this," she said.

I gave her a reassuring hug. "No, but I'm not going to walk out on you now! But can I just ask you to clarify something: is Bill really your brother rather than your husband?"

She laughed, "Of course he's my brother, I told you that! The husband and wife arrangement was simply a cover, but I did not count on meeting you," and she kissed me very tenderly.

The world seemed to stand still for a few seconds, and all I could say was "I feel the same."

"Let's give it time and see what happens," Jill said.

We walked a bit further along the cliff path hand in hand, before pausing to look out to sea and simply enjoying the moment.

On our return to the house, Jill and I joined Bill and Sue in the lounge.

"We can tell you a little more," said Bill, "but the less you know, the less you can give away, if you're ever questioned."

"That sounds ominous," I muttered.

"Bill and Jill had to hide their past. On paper, they are dead, having been killed in a car crash, but now, people are suspicious," Sue explained, "and they want confirmation of whether they are dead or alive. I can't say more," she added.

"Thank you, at least I'm a bit more in the picture," I said.

We went on to discuss the other car, the black Range Rover, and then Jill said to Bill, "If you are busy tomorrow, Ray and I could go to the log cabin. It's safe and very private. Would you like to go, Ray?" she turned to me.

"Yes, of course," I replied, and Bill agreed. A few minutes later, we made our goodbyes, and I drove back to the hotel.

In my room, I rang Mike and told him everything. He thanked me, saying that it was useful and gave him more to go on. "I may be free tomorrow late afternoon," he said, "and, if so, I'll come and see you."

He rang off, and I sat thinking about all that had happened, and considering how a lovely lady's life had been put in this precarious position all because she had followed her brother to the UK. She hadn't had any choice in leaving, I thought, with their country's regime and attitude. I was determined to help Jill as much as I could. With that concluding thought, I got ready for bed.

CHAPTER 8

The chase hastens

In an area enclosed by a high stone wall topped with electrified wires, a man and a dog kept a constant patrol. The entrance had high metal gates and an intercom, with camera, for those wishing to gain admittance.

Inside, was the headquarters of a secret Russian organisation. It was run by a man in his late 50s. He had piercing blue eyes, grey hair, a pleasant face, and black-rimmed glasses. He was seated at a large leather desk conversing with two others: a younger man and a woman. The grey-haired man was asking the other man if he had heard from the agents who had reported seeing the woman they all thought was dead. They had spotted her in the UK, of all places.

"No, sir, we've heard nothing further," the man replied, "our agents seem to have disappeared. Mind you, they've always been loose cannons."

"Well, keep me updated," the grey-haired man said.

When he got back to his office, the younger man made a phone call, "Get Alexei and Ivan's chalet checked, and report back," he ordered, and hung up. Perhaps they hadn't really seen the woman and it was a false alarm. It all needed checking out though, or Popov would explode. He was well known for showing no mercy if his people made a mistake.

The grey-haired man, Colonel Popov, looked out of the window. What would the embassy chief say about the missing agents, he wondered. He sighed, things had been easier when it had been the KGB. This FBS had more departments, and there was so much overlap and confusion. Ah well, he said to himself, we will see this afternoon when I go to London. At least I haven't had a message to meet the British colonel near London Bridge - a sign that the Brits wanted something or had got something to trade.

A black limousine and bodyguards picked Popov up at 1.30pm, and he set off for the London Embassy.

Colonel Popov entered the Embassy and took the lift up to a room he used when he stayed there. There was to be a reception that evening which would be attended by two British ambassadors, both men he knew well. Perhaps I can squeeze some information out of them, he thought.

He poured a drink and was just about to sit down and enjoy it when his phone rang. It was an embassy secretary asking if he could go and see his boss immediately. He replied that he could, knocked back his drink, grabbed some folders, and made his way down in the lift to the ambassador's office on the ground floor. The secretary recognised him and told him to go straight in; the ambassador was waiting for him. A large man was seated behind a leather desk. His short greying black hair was receding, and he wore rimless glasses, a white shirt and black suit, a tie, and he was smoking a cigar.

"Well, Popov, what is this about a dead Russian woman actually being alive and well in the UK? Is it true? I thought we were sure that she had been killed in a car accident in Germany two or three years ago. What is going on?" He asked in a gruff voice.

"Ambassador, it has not been confirmed yet," Popov replied, "We have sent two agents to investigate, but we are having trouble reaching them at the moment. Either they have been detained by MI5 or have had something else. We're checking into it right this minute. It was a passing car they spotted this person in, so we have some way yet to go before we can be certain who it is," he continued, "I intend to try and get any information I can from your British guests tonight, and, in the meantime, I have got agents searching the chalet park."

"I see," was the reply from the ambassador, "well, keep me informed."

The two of them went on to discuss the evening reception and other embassy matters. When Popov finally left the ambassador, it was nearly time for him get ready for the reception. As he was making his way back to his room, he took his mobile out and rang the young man he had spoken to about the disappearing agents. He wanted an update. He was told that agents had checked for accidents and none had been reported. They still did not know the location of Alexei and Ivan, but the chalet park had been checked and cleared of their belongings.

"OK," Popov said, "do let me know if anything further comes to light."

The agent agreed and added that they'd hopefully have more news the following day.

At the MI5 offices in London, a meeting was being held in an office belonging to a top official, someone who was responsible for coordinating missions like agents being caught and detained, and then reporting back to the head of this organisation. Sue was there, and the two of them were discussing their position and what to do with the agents.

"They have nothing," Sue said, "and they're old hands who know we can't hold them forever without charge."

"Yes," said the official, "but we must be sure that they did not get a chance to pass sensitive information further up the chain."

"We're working on it," Sue said, "and I'll report back as soon as we have something."

Sue left the office and the official called the ambassador and put her in the picture in case she ended up being questioned at the reception she was attending at the Russian Embassy.

Popov was smartly dressed in his uniform. The British

ambassador would be sitting near him, so he was ready to question her. This stinks of MI5, he thought. He entered the large dining room, and, like everyone else, was announced as he came in: Colonel Popov, head of the overseas department of the FBS. He shook hands with the Russian host and his wife, and then made his way down the long table in the centre of the room to the place he knew to be his. There were several people already seated, including the British ambassador on his left. They acknowledged each other and sat down, ready for things to begin.

Popov decided to leave his questioning until after the main course when several glasses of wine had been enjoyed. After ordering another glass of wine for the British ambassador, he smiled, made a bit of small talk about the food, and then asked quietly, "May I ask you if you are aware of any of my agents being picked up by special branch?"

"No," she said, appearing surprised, "have you lost some then?"

"Nobody in particular," Popov replied, "I'm just wondering about rumours regarding your special branch being active."

"I haven't heard anything," the British ambassador said, "but if anything has happened then it would be above board and legal, as I'm sure you realise. Your people would be notified in due course." She turned away to talk to her colleague. Popov grunted unhappily, that hadn't got him very far. Perhaps it was a cat and mouse game with MI5.

CHAPTER 9

Trying to get back to normal

I was at Cliff House by 9 am. The Range Rover was ready to go, with food in a hamper in the boot and the driver ready in the driver's seat. Jill was dressed in slacks and shirt, along with a sun hat and dark glasses. We embraced before making ourselves comfortable on the back seat. We made small talk as we sped along the coast road. Before we knew it, we had arrived at the log cabin. We parked, entered the cabin, put the food in the fridge, and decided to have a refreshing cup of tea before heading off to the beach.

We sat out on the veranda with our tea.

"Do you look the same now as you did in Russia?" I asked, "Or have you changed your appearance?"

"More or less," she replied.

"I just wondered if you had dyed your hair or cut it differently to disguise yourself a bit. Would it be worth trying to change something?"

"That's not a bad idea," she said, as if she'd never thought about it, "I could get some wigs."

"Well, from what I can tell, they're looking for you as you were back then, using photos from your past, so if you change your appearance, then it will at least make it harder for them."

She said that she would talk to Sue about it.

"What I don't understand," I said, "is why they are after you, but Bill is free to come and go wherever and whenever he wants too. Why aren't they after him? Or why haven't they recognised him? He's out and about all the time!"

"He's had some work done," Jill explained, "and he's also grown a beard. He blends in well with other men in his age group. Also, you may have noticed, we don't tend to go out together much, and we certainly don't have the same interests," and with that, she took the tray of crockery back to the kitchen.

We set off along the path to the beach.

"I think it would be a good idea to stay here on cliff, rather than go down on the beach, I said, pointing out an area under some trees which was dappled with shade, "it will be cool and private."

As Jill took our things over to the shady patch, I walked down the steps to the beach hut where I knew I'd find a couple of deckchairs. I carried them back up the steps and positioned them under the trees. We sat down, removed our sun hats, and enjoyed the cool shade and the sea air that was scented with the blossoms and flowers around us. We sat close together, holding hands and silent. I broke the silence by remarking how calm the sea looked today, adding "It's lovely sitting here, plus it's impossible to see us from above."

Jill agreed, and we sat in silence for a few minutes again.

"Have you thought about the future at all?" I asked.

Jill looked surprised, "No," she said.

"I was just wondering if you're happy living as you are, or whether you have plans to build a more normal life, perhaps with a relationship?"

Jill smiled, "Why? Do you think I have somebody in mind?"

I laughed, "Well, I hoped..."

She snorted with laughter, "Well, I wonder who it would be!"

I leaned over and kissed her, whispering "me" as we broke apart.

"We obviously feel the same way," Jill said, "but we have to get our present situation sorted out first."

"I know," I replied, "but sometimes it's good to say how you feel and know where you stand."

"True," she agreed.

I looked at my watch and suggested we go back to the cabin to have lunch. We left the chairs where they were, got up, and walked back to the cabin, each holding a handle of the heavy hamper.

"Just a couple of sandwiches for me, please," Jill said.

"I'm not very hungry either, but I will have a glass of wine. Will you join me?" I asked.

Jill nodded and then poured us a glass each.

We sat at the table on the veranda to enjoy our sandwiches and wine.

"Do you have any idea what sort of life you'd like after this is all sorted out?" I asked.

"A life like this," she replied, "like we are now. A life where we can go where we want and do what we want, and I want a garden with roses in it," she added.

We laughed.

After lunch, we tidied up and then walked back to our deckchairs on the cliff.

"I think we can risk going down onto the beach now," said Jill. She was standing at the top of the steps. "It's so quiet down there."

I agreed and I folded and carried our deckchairs down onto the beach, Jill following behind.

We sunbathed, sitting and talking about a rosy future where we'd both be free to go anywhere we wanted to. I also mentioned how we could continue our relationship after I returned home, deciding that we could meet halfway and spend a few days together on a regular basis. It was good to be positive.

I decided to use the beach hut to change into my swimming shorts, and Jill stripped off her outerwear to reveal a bikini. Hand-in-hand, we walked down to the sea for a refreshing swim: two mature people acting like young lovers. We revelled in each other's company.

After our dip, we dried ourselves off with towels before returning to our deckchairs. The sun was strong, and we were soon bone-dry.

"I don't want to burn," Jill said, as she got dressed again, and I decided to change too. We shared a bottle of water. Suddenly, the peace was shattered by Jill's mobile ringing.

"Yes, yes, of course," she said. She sighed and looked at me sadly. "Bill would like us to get back to the house. Sue is there, and she wants to talk to us all."

"Perhaps she just wants to know how we are, how you're coping," I said, trying to reassure Jill as the driver took us back to Cliff House.

"Yes," she said, "You know that I could not cope with all this without you, Ray," she added.

I looked at her. Her eyes were full of love. I smiled and cuddled up close to her. She lay her head on my shoulder.

A few minutes later, we were in the lounge. Sue and Bill sat on the settee and Jill and I took the armchairs.

"Sorry to rush you here and spoil your day," Sue said, "but events are moving a bit, so I need to talk to you all together. First, it appears after questioning the two agents, that although they know the make, model and colour of your car, they had not taken note of your number plate. They had a blown-up photo of Jill in their possession, to check that the woman they had seen was actually her, but they hadn't managed to get close enough to check. We were careful in our questioning, so as not to make it obvious that we were protecting her. We just made out that we were interested in why Russian agents were tailing British citizens."

Jill breathed out with relief.

"However, we still need to be very careful as their HQ think that Jill and Bill are in this area. I think that they are committed to tracking you down." Sue explained, "so you can only go to places we know are safe, and you need to be accompanied."

"What about if Jill disguises herself?" I asked.

Sue said that she'd think on that.

"And are these people armed? I need to know," I added, "if I'm to be prepared to protect us both."

"Well, some are, but usually only embassy bodyguards."

"OK, thank you," I said, and then told the three of them that I needed to get back to the hotel to get ready for dinner with Mike.

"That's fine," Sue said, "and perhaps I'll see you at dinner," she smiled.

On my arrival back at the hotel, the receptionist handed me a note. It was from Mike letting me know that he'd meet me in the bar near the dining room at 6.45 pm. I just had time to shower and change before heading down to the bar. Mike walked in and greeted me with a handshake. The waiter showed us to our table, which was near the front window, allowing me to see who entered the hotel. We declined starters and ordered steak. I gave Mike a quick update on the conversation I'd had with Sue earlier that day. I'd just finished when the woman herself asked if she could join us. We both smiled and nodded, and I gestured to the spare chair at our table. "I'll have what they're having!" Sue called to our waiter.

I poured us a glass of wine each and then turned to Sue, "What do you think will happen now? Is Jill in danger?"

"Yes, unfortunately, she is," Sue said, "as long as they still think there's a chance it's her they saw. They know that they'll be able to use her as a lever to get at Bill," she explained, "But, I have a plan that I will put in place tomorrow. If Jill changes her looks, we might just be able to convince them that they were mistaken." She looked at me and then Mike, "So, no commando stuff, Ray and Mike, let's see if my plan works before you men decide on something more drastic!"

"Us?" Mike said laughing, "Never!"

We tucked into our steaks and enjoyed our evening.

CHAPTER 10
Things begin to sort out

Sue was briefing three of her agents: one woman and two men. The woman looked very similar to Jill.

"I want you to go to the chalet park," Sue said, "where the Russian agents were staying. I want you to be seen, and for them to think that they were mistaken in thinking they saw Jill. I have no doubt that Colonel Popov has agents in the area carrying out surveillance, waiting for a sighting, so we're going to give them one. You have radio backing and a van nearby to call on if needed." Sue turned to other two, "All three of you are better trained than any of Popov's agents, I'm sure."

The three agents confirmed that they understood their instructions and had read the file.

A little later, the three agents arrived at the chalet park in a grey car and parked in the car park there. There were several other vehicles, including a van parked in the corner. The female agent got out with one of the men, and they walked down onto the beach hand-in-hand. They strolled along, paddling in the shallows until they reached the cliff jutting out to sea. Then, they turned around and walked back along the base of the cliff, by the beach huts and holidaymakers. They carried on up the slope to the shop, and the man went in to buy ice creams. The woman stood outside, looking in the shop window. A man dressed in jeans and a short-sleeved shirt approached and greeted her with a "hello" as he walked past. She looked at him through her sunglasses and returned his greeting. He walked off towards the car park. Her companion came out of the shop and handed her an ice cream. They made their way back to the car park. The woman noticed the man who had spoken to her. He was sitting in a black car with a woman.

She spoke under her breath into her hidden radio: "I have been eyeballed, black car." Then she and her fellow agent got into their car and pulled out of the car park, onto the road. The black car pulled out not long after them.

"Looks like we have company," she reported.

"Just keep going. Drive to the hotel and do exactly as you were instructed," said the voice on the radio.

"I think they're the man and woman we're looking for," the man in the black car reported into his radio. "We'll keep their car just in sight," he added.

"And we have surveillance on the van in front of you in case that's also following them," said the voice on the radio."

"OK, and if we need any help, we'll call for it." The man said, "I'm hoping we'll get the opportunity to approach this couple and ask them questions."

"But don't do anything to arouse their suspicions," said the voice on the radio.

"I know," said the man, "and you make sure to keep back, we don't want them to realise they're being followed by a convoy!"

The grey car with the blond woman and two men in it arrived at the hotel and parked. The three of them went in, heading to the bar. There, they found a table close to another unoccupied table. The man who'd been the driver went up to the bar to order drinks, returning with three a few minutes later.

A man and woman entered the bar and sat at the neighbouring table. The man went up to the bar.

"Excuse me," said the woman, leaning over to the Jill look-alike, "are you local?"

"No," replied "Jill", "we're just on holiday for a few days, exploring this coast a bit. We haven't seen much yet, really just the chalet park and the areas around there. Are you looking for somewhere?"

"Nowhere in particular," replied the woman, "I was just going to ask if you could recommend places to visit."

Her companion returned with drinks, "Making friends already, eh?" he asked, "I'm Bob, and this is Jane," he added.

"I'm Chris, and my friends are Dan and Fred," said the woman acting as Jill.

The conversation was being recorded by the two radio vans parked discreetly nearby. The conversation seemed like a normal conversation between two groups of people who had just met on holiday. It lasted about twenty minutes, and then the couple from the black car left and drove out of the car park.

The Jill look-alike reported their departure and the voice on the radio informed her that a car had gone after them: "You two stay at the hotel until you get the all-clear," the female voice on the radio added.

Popov was sitting at his desk, reading reports when his phone rang.

"Popov," he said into it.

He listened and then replied, "Come to my office now."

Within a few minutes, there was a knock on his door. A man entered. Popov gestured to a chair, and the man took a seat.

"Well, what's happened?" asked Popov.

The man gave him a full report, relating how the blond woman had returned to the chalet park. "This time, the agent had a good look at her and even followed and spoke to her. She is not the woman we're looking for," he added, "she just looks similar. She's just a holidaymaker here with her partner and brother."

"It sounds like your unreliable agents were wrong, then," said Popov, "but have you compared the photos that were taken the other day with ones taken today, just to make sure?" he asked.

"Yes, and she looks the same," the man replied. "Our agents did the right thing in asking for it all to be checked," he added, "and they did an excellent job questioning the woman and her companions. This was simply a false alarm. However, we'll keep looking for Alexei and Ivan, and they will be spoken to about jumping to conclusions."

"Remove this situation from the urgent list, then, please," Popov said.

The man nodded, then left the office.

Popov asked his PA to get the Russian ambassador on the phone. She quickly came back to him, "The ambassador is on the line," she said.

"I just wanted to update you and let you know that our agents have verified that the woman they saw was not the one they first thought it was," he explained.

"Good, so the case is closed then. Thank you."

The ambassador hung up, and Popov put the phone down.

"We shall see," he muttered, and lit a cigar, "yes, we shall see."

CHAPTER 11

The dust settles

I was ready early and so decided to go down to the hotel beach. I located an umbrella to sit under and, having brought my binoculars along, scanned the beach and cliff top. I had just finished my first sweep when a voice to the side of me said "hello". It was the local man whom I had spoken to about the cove. He explained that he had sailed his boat into the cove and explored two of the caves, but found nothing unusual. He thought that the yacht just used it to anchor in for protection against the weather.

"Well, at least that answers that. It's just that one time I saw lights near there," I said.

"Maybe, it was just youngsters messing about," he said.

"Probably," I said, and thanked him. He walked off, waving goodbye as he went.

I scanned the sea, beach and cliff top once more. No yacht and nothing untoward. I had finished when I spotted the flash of the sun catching glass in the long grass on top of the cliff. Funny, I thought, who could be up there? I went back to my room at the hotel and did yet another sweep of the cliff top from my balcony. From that angle, I could see someone lying in the long grass with binoculars aimed at the beach. It could be a birdwatcher, I thought, but best to be safe than sorry. I called Sue, who said to leave it with her.

I had just hung up when my mobile rang; it was Jill. "Would you like to come over and have a sandwich with me here?" she said, "then we can decide where to go this afternoon." I agreed.

Fifteen minutes later, I was parking outside Cliff House. The butler let me in and showed me into the lounge, where I sat on the settee. Before long, a woman with collar-length black hair, bright red lipstick and black-rimmed glasses entered the room. I recognised Jill's smile and mannerisms, but realised that it would be difficult to recognise her from a distance or if you didn't know her well.

"You look just as beautiful," I said, and Jill smiled.

The butler brought in a tray with sandwiches and two glasses of wine. Jill joined me on the settee, and we tucked into the sandwiches. "Have you shown Sue your new look?" I asked.

"Yes, we did a video call," she said, "she was pleased with it, but it will take me a while to get used to it."

I changed the subject, then, to our plans for the afternoon.

In her office, Sue took a call from an MI5 operative who dealt with phone tapping and radio signals. He explained that they'd picked up a call to the Russian Embassy regarding Sue's case: Jill. Sue was relieved to hear that the Russians no longer considered their sighting to be of Jill and the matter was now off their urgent list. Sue thanked the operative and rang her boss, who was happy that Sue's idea had worked, then she called Jill: "It's good news," Sue said, "but let's not get ahead of ourselves. Keep everything the same for a while and only go to the areas we talked about."

When Jill relayed her conversation with Sue to me, I was pleased and relieved. "Hopefully, in the not too distant future we'll be able to go to other places together without fear of being recognised," I said, "but I guess today will be at the log cabin again, yes?"

Jill nodded, "If it's OK with you," she said.

The driver took us both to the cabin. We opened up and left the driver there while we headed off to the shady area on the cliff top. I went and fetched the deck chairs, and we sat close together, both of us happy that things were getting better and looking forward to a brighter future together. We talked about the places we would like to visit together: the theatre, cinema and restaurants, and hoped that we'd be able to go soon.

"It's like a heavy weight has been lifted off our shoulders," I said to Jill, and she agreed. We sat and chatted about the future for an hour or so, and then decided it was time we returned to Cliff House. I took the deckchairs back to the hut, and then we walked back to the cabin. The driver put our things in the boot, and we drove off.

The journey back went quickly. Jill asked if I'd like to go into the house for a drink, and I agreed. As we entered the house, she ordered tea off the butler, and we went into the lounge.

Jill seemed the most relaxed I'd ever seen her, as we sat on the settee and waited for the tea to arrive. I asked after Bill, and she told me that he'd be on his way home soon. I changed the subject back to places we'd discussed at the cliff top, places we wanted to visit together: "Further up the coast, in the Cromer area, there are one or two places I'd like to visit and things I'd like to show you," I said, "Cromer pier, for example."

"I've never been," she said, "sounds like a plan!"

"Well, we can put it to Sue and Bill, and see what they think," I said.

"Oh yes, run it past the wise ones!" she laughed.

We were still laughing when Bill walked in.

"I've heard the good news from Sue," he said, after he'd greeted us both, "it's good news indeed."

"Yes," said Jill, "it certainly is."

Bill's mobile vibrated, and he excused himself for a minute. When he came back, he told us that Sue was coming over tonight and wanted to see all three of us. The butler brought in the tea tray and poured out three cups.

"When you go out," he said, "you should still keep using the Range Rover and driver for a while."

"No problem," I said.

"Why don't we have a fish and chip dinner tonight from the Chippy?" He suggested, and said that he'd get the butler to organise a gazebo in the garden so that we could enjoy our food outside. "It's beautiful weather at the moment, so we ought to make the most of it," he added.

Jill and I agreed, and I added that I needed to go back to the hotel to freshen up and change. We agreed on 6.45 pm for the meal, and I made my goodbyes, kissing Jill on the cheek.

When I got back to my room, I rang Mike and updated him on all that had happened. He was pleased and commented that Sue's idea had been a good one. "Soon, I'm sure, Jill will be free to enjoy her life properly," he added. He thanked me for the update and rang off.

I then called my PA and was relieved to hear that all was well back at the office. "I'm thinking of adding a few more days onto my holiday," I told her, and she assured me that she could hold the fort. "Just have a good time," she said, and we brought the call to an end.

With that bit of admin done, I showered and changed. I was just moving my wallet and keys into my clean trousers when my mobile rang; it was Jill.

"I'm glad I caught you," she said: "I'm sending the car to pick you up, so you can relax and have a drink."

"Perfect," I said, "thank you."

She informed me that the driver was leaving now.

By the time I'd got my things together and walked down to the hotel entrance, the car was just pulling up. The driver dropped me off at Cliff House and zoomed off to collect the fish and chips. I was greeted at the front door by the butler and escorted through the house to the rear garden, where there was a gazebo with a table and chairs set out in it.

Sue, Jill and Bill were sitting there, and I greeted them. Bill gestured to a seat and then handed me a glass of wine. I complimented Jill on their beautiful garden as I admired the multitude of bedding plants and bushes that were filling the air with their scent. Conversation flowed easily as we were all more relaxed now, a change from the gloom of yesterday, and it was all thanks to Sue.

I thanked her again and spoke of my hope of enjoying new places further afield with Jill, now that the threat was gone.

"It does look like the Russians have accepted that the woman they saw was not Jill, but I know Colonel Popov, their head of intelligence, and he will keep a skeleton staff here a bit longer to keep an eye out," she explained, "so Jill's lookalike will remain in the area of the Chalet Park and nearby, so please keep away from there for the time being."

"OK, good idea," I said, "and we'd like to try and visit Cromer and see an afternoon matinee on the pier, if that's OK."

Sue said she didn't see why not, as long as Jill wore her disguise.

The butler entered the room with our fish and chips, and we tucked in enthusiastically. We finished the meal with a fruit salad and cream, followed by coffee. Then Jill asked me to accompany her on an evening walk. She asked Sue and Bill to join us, but they declined. Jill smiled at me; it was obvious that she was pleased it would be just the two of us.

Colonel Popov was sorting out papers to take home, as he was out on a visit the next day. This done, he emailed the department looking into the missing agents and ordered them to keep an eye on the chalet park area for a couple of days. He put the papers in his case, ordered his car, and lit a cigar. As he exhaled, he thought about the missing agents and how the situation reeked of MI5 involvement. A voice over the intercom told him that his car was waiting, so he stood up, made his way outside and slumped in the back seat of the car, still puffing his cigar.

Jill and I left the house and walked along the cliff top path. There was a lovely sea breeze and I could taste the salt in the air. It was dusk, but we could still see the beach and the waves lapping against the shore. Jill held my hand and snuggled up to me, saying, "We may have a chance to act like normal couples do soon, and get away from the usual safe places, and Bill too."

"Yes," I said, "I really want to take you to a show at Cromer, I'm sure you would like it!"

She squeezed my hand and nodded.

We stopped and looked down at the beach. "This is idyllic.," I said, drawing her closer for a kiss.

"Yes," she breathed, as we broke apart. "I know it will take time to adjust to being normal," she said, "but I think we can be patient and enjoy the experience." She kissed me again and then we walked slowly back to the house.

The butler let us in and advised us that Sue and Bill were in the lounge. They were seated in the armchairs, so we took the settee.

"Coffee's on its way," Bill said, "We've been talking about your idea of going to see the show on the pier," he continued, "and we think it's do-able, but you need to take two of Sue's men. Just to be on the safe side," he added, "if anything happens..."

The butler brought in a large pot of coffee, along with sugar, milk and biscuits. I waited for him to leave, and then told Bill that I didn't see a problem with his and Sue's recommendation. Jill agreed with me. Over coffee, we agreed to set off the next morning at 9.30. Jill seemed happy and excited.

After coffee, I asked Bill to arrange for his driver to take me back, and Sue asked if she could come back with me as she was staying at the hotel that night. "Of course," I said. We all went to the front door. Sue shook hands with Bill and Jill, Bill shook my hand, and Jill kissed me on the cheek.

"You and Jill seem quite serious," Sue commented on the ride back, "I wish you all the best for your future together."

"Thank you," I said.

At the hotel, we went our separate ways. Mike had left me a message at reception asking me to give him a call, which I did from my mobile when I had got back to my room.

"Hi Ray, I just thought I would ring to make sure you're OK and to advise you not to rush into things too fast." He said.

I laughed and then told him what we'd arranged for the following day. He commented that it sounded good and then rang off. I decided to sit out on the balcony for a while, as it was still hot and I wanted to wind down a bit before bed. As I sat there, I decided that I would ask Jill whether she could imagine a future with me, once things got back to normal, and what that future would entail. After deciding on that, I left the balcony, slid the door shut, and went to bed.

There was an email waiting for Popov by the time he got home. It was from the department dealing with the missing agents, informing him that they had arranged a 24-hour cover of the chalet park area to keep an eye out for the three in the grey car. Well, he thought to himself, it's best to be sure, and it would also be good to know what had happened to the agents. He poured himself a drink and sat in his armchair thinking about the last two days and all that had happened. A woman's voice cut into his thoughts: "Dinner's ready, dear. Don't let it get cold." He stood up, put his glass down, and shouted, "Coming, dear!"

Sue rang her people to check everything had been put in place for the Jill lookalike and the two men to stay for three nights and to behave like holidaymakers. All had been arranged, she was happy to be told, and they knew exactly what to do. She retired for the night.

At 9.15 am the next morning, I was at Cliff house. An excited Jill greeted me with a peck on the cheek and pulled me into the library, where Bill was sitting. I asked him if he was coming with us, and he shook his head, explaining that he had a busy day ahead of him. "You two enjoy yourselves, though," he added.

Jill and I got into the car, and I checked that I had my binoculars in my bag, I did. The two bodyguards got in the front, and we set off on the A149. Soon, we were going through Wells-next-the-Sea, and I started pointing out things to Jill. I was happy to be exploring the area that I'd come on holiday to see! At Blakeney, we found a good place to stop to have a drink and get some fresh air. We both felt relaxed as we stretched our legs around the car park area and had a quick coffee in a café. The bodyguards seemed quite happy to stay in the car with their bottles of water. We then set off again on the same road and eventually came to Sherringham. There, I asked the driver to park as near as he could to the seafront so that I could show Jill around. As it was lunchtime, I asked if she wanted to find somewhere to have something to eat. Jill declined, saying that she'd prefer to eat at Cromer. It was only about thirty minutes away now, so I agreed. After another stretch of our legs, we set off once again, driving through the Runtons and on to Cromer, where we parked in a public car park.

Jill and I set off down the main street, towards the shopping area by the church to have a look around. Jill mentioned that she liked it. We had a snacky lunch in a café I knew.

"Ray, I am really enjoying this," Jill said, "I feel like a different person doing this."

"Well, I hope you enjoy the afternoon performance on the pier," I said, "I have booked tickets for us."

She smiled, "I enjoy everything we do together."

I smiled back.

We finished our lunch, and I took her for a walk along the front, then we decided to walk along the beach to make our way back. People were swimming in the sea, for it was the perfect day to enjoy the beach and sea.

"It's a shame we didn't bring our cozzies," I said, and Jill agreed.

After people-watching for a time, we went up the slope near the pier area. It was nearly time for the show. We walked slowly, hand-in-hand along the planking of the pier until we came to the theatre doors. I gave my name to the attendant and collected our tickets. We were escorted into the theatre and shown to our seats in the second row, near the front. Jill looked so excited! I squeezed her hand, and then we settled down to enjoy the show.

The show was as good as I remembered, with dancing girls, comedians, and singers – the perfect variety show. Jill really did love it, laughing and clapping enthusiastically. It lasted two hours and was worth every penny I'd paid for the tickets.

Bill had managed to get home early and was sitting in the

library, sorting and signing papers. The butler knocked on the door, opened it and informed Bill that Sue was there to see him. Sue entered the room, apologising for disturbing Bill: "I just wanted to catch you to talk about Jill and Ray," she said, "I think it's clear that they are very much in love. But what will you do if they stay together and want to settle down?"

"Well, I would give them my blessing, and I'm sure the paperwork could be sorted out for us to divorce," Bill said, "Do you think things can work out for them?"

"Yes, I can find a way to give Jill a past here in the UK that would stand up to scrutiny, and let's face it, she has got into this trouble by supporting you. If she's not with you any more, then that removes most of the danger. I think she deserves a better life, don't you?"

"I just hope that we have completely fooled Popov," said Bill, "he's a very stubborn man."

"I hope so too," said Sue.

"I'm going to invite them both to go to the festival on Saturday," Bill said, "can you organise your side of things? It will do them good, and I have a ticket for Ray's friend Mike to attend."

"Yes, I can organise it," said Sue, "and I'll be there too. It should be a good day, and a good way of getting Jill used to mixing with people again. She can't spend the rest of her life hiding or looking over her shoulder." Sue ended the conversation by inviting Bill to dinner that night at the hotel and asking him to pass on her invitation to Ray and Jill. Jill and I came out of the pier theatre, having both enjoyed the experience. It had definitely been worth the journey to see it. Jill phoned the bodyguards to say we were on the way to the car park to head back home.

As we approached the road to the car park, her mobile rang. It was Bill.

"Bill's got us tickets for the festival on Saturday," she explained after she'd hung up, "he's got a ticket for Mike too, if you could let him know. And Sue has invited Bill and us for dinner tonight at the hotel."

"Great," I said, "I can let Mike know."

The bodyguards were waiting for us at the car, and we made good time getting back to Cliff House. I took my things out of the boot of the Range Rover and transferred them to the boot of my car, before heading into the house for a cup of tea before I left. On our way to the lounge, Jill popped her head around the door of the library to let Bill know we were back.

The cup of tea was a wonderful refreshment after our car journey and we just sat on the settee enjoying it.

Bill put his head around the door and asked if we'd enjoyed our trip and the show. Excitedly, Jill started telling him all about it, so Bill came in and sat down. After Jill had finished, Bill told us about all the dignitaries who were coming to the festival and what would be at the festival. I asked about the dress code, which I was informed was smart casual, and Bill went on to explain that the festival was an annual event and that it was important because it brought business to this area and gave everyone a chance to get better acquainted, and a chance to mix and relax.

"You mentioned embassy staff, though. Why do they come?" I asked.

"Well, a lot of the businesses are big exporters, and the embassies often get involved in dealing with the contracts," Bill explained.

"Why has Sue invited us to join her for dinner?" asked Jill.

"No reason," Bill replied "probably just to say thank you for following her orders."

I finished my tea and made my farewells, saying that I'd got a call to make back at the hotel. Jill saw me out and kissed me on the cheek.

"See you later," she said.

PART THREE

CHAPTER 12

The unforgiving

I parked in my usual place at the hotel and went up to my room to call Mike. He didn't answer, so I left him a message about the festival ticket and the arrangements, explaining that I'd meet him there. I also rang my PA for a daily update; all was well.

As I sat on my balcony, the events of the last few days ran through my mind. What's next? I thought. I really hoped that everything would be OK now that the danger was over for Jill. I gave a sigh of relief and then showered and changed.

Popov had finished his meal and was sat smoking a cigar in his garden. He still didn't feel quite right about the blond woman; something was niggling him. He'd put it to the back of his mind until after the festival, he decided. Then, he changed his mind and called the supervisor in charge of the operation, ordering him to send more people to the festival and for them to keep their eyes and ears open as he still thought MI5 was involved. He'd been in the game a long time and knew when to follow his instinct. Something did not feel right.

The supervisor knew better than to question any of Popov's orders and so arranged for another two agents to attend the festival. "We also have a college friend of the blond lady at HQ, so she could attend the festival and look out for her," he said.

Popov was pleased with what had been arranged. He took a sip of his brandy and sat there smiling to himself. Well, he thought, MI5 might think they can pull the wool over my eyes, but they have a lot more to learn about me before they can do that. He sat back blowing smoke in the night air.

After leaving Bill, Sue contacted her team and arranged for agents to attend the festival. She was convinced that something was wrong now, that Popov had accepted things all too easily. She was also surprised that there'd been no reaction from him after two of his agents had been charged with past offences. He's up to something, she thought. However, Sue had no intention of voicing her worries to Ray and Jill at the moment. It was all just speculation. Let's hope I'm wrong, she thought.

Sue thought that Jill's disguise would stand up to anyone's observation, from any distance, unless they knew her well and knew her mannerisms, her voice, and her way of moving. Satisfied with what she had arranged, Sue changed her focus to what to wear for the evening ahead, and began to get ready for dinner. When I got to the hotel dining room, Sue, Jill and Bill were already seated at the table and there was a wine bucket, complete with wine, on the table. I sat in the chair next to Jill and said good evening to everybody. Bill poured us all a glass of wine, and we raised and clinked glasses, saying "cheers".

The waiter came and took our orders.

Bill suddenly raised his glass. "Let's raise our glasses to Ray and Sue for their help and friendship over these last two weeks. Thank you, both, from both of us," he said. I returned the toast, saying, "My help is my pleasure, but it's Sue who has been the one to take most of it on her shoulders, so let's give a toast to Sue, then we'd better order more wine," I laughed and everyone joined in..

By the time we'd finished our meals, a band had started to play. Glen Miller's "in the mood" began, and I asked Jill if she'd like to dance.

"I'll try," she said.

We managed a kind of foxtrot type of dance. We weren't

very good at all, but we enjoyed it. We danced to a couple of songs and then rested while Sue and Bill attempted a jive.

A bit later, the band played some slower numbers which we enjoyed more.

"Are you enjoying the evening?" I asked Jill.

"Tremendously," she answered, "I thought I'd forgotten how to dance!"

We then decided to get some fresh air by going for a walk. I told Bill and Sue where we were going, and then we made our way out of the hotel, along the path and down to the beach. There we sat beside each other on one of the sunbeds, gazing up at the stars. I put my arm around Jill's shoulders, and she snuggled close to me.

"Perhaps for the first time in my life, fate has been good to me by allowing us to meet and fall in love," I said.

"Love? That's the first time you have said that word to me," she said, smiling. We kissed tenderly and then she pulled me even closer for a stronger and more lingering kiss. We're in love with each other, I thought.

I noticed that another couple had come down to the beach and were kissing. I looked at Jill, "I think it's time to move on," I said, gesturing to the other couple. She laughed and nodded. We took a walk along the sand, at the sea's edge for a few paces, before realising that neither of us was wearing the right shoes for that. We turned around and walked back up the path to the hotel.

We stole one last kiss before entering hotel reception and making our way to the dinning room. Bill and Sue were sitting at the table talking. As we came up to them, Sue smiled and told us that we made a lovely couple.

"Let's hope we can carry on like this," I said, "and that nothing will part us." We held hands.

Bill announced that it was time for him and Jill to make a move now, so Sue and I walked them out into the car park. I gave a wave, and then they were gone.

Sue turned to me, "Goodnight, Ray, try to keep hoping," she said, and then headed off to her room.

I returned to mine where I couldn't help wondering what the future did actually hold. I couldn't help worrying. Had the Russians really been fooled? I wasn't sure. Although I had hoped that Jill would be able to lead a normal life without looking over her shoulder all the time, I was beginning to think that there would always be a risk, it would always be in the background. Jill was worth it all, though, I concluded.

CHAPTER 13

A taste of freedom

Another day began, and Jill rang early to ask me to go shopping with her as she needed a new outfit for the festival.

We had arranged to meet at her house at 10 am, giving us both time to sort ourselves out. This would be the first time that Jill had been shopping like this for a long time and luckily she did not have a favourite shop she frequented, so there was no danger of shop assistants seeing through her disguise.

I arrived at Cliff House just before 10 am, and the Range Rover was already ready and waiting for us.

We set off, and on the way, Jill told me that she couldn't remember the last time she'd been able to go shopping like this. She explained that Sue had advised her on where to go, and soon we were parking outside a rather upmarket looking boutique called "Femmes". We went in, and were greeted by the manager; no doubt she had been informed of Jill's intended visit. The place had money oozing out of the walls, and there was good service with nothing too much bother. There were several women trying on clothes and receiving the kind of attention only these types of places could afford to provide. Jill started trying on dresses. I waited patiently, and each time she came out of the changing room, I gave feedback on whether I liked it or not. I knew nothing about fashion, but I knew what I liked Jill in, and it was lovely to see Jill happy and enjoying herself.

Eventually, Jill had made her choice, and the outfit was boxed up for her, and the driver took it to the car.

"I bet there's a nice café somewhere, so why don't we get some sandwiches and a drink. It's about lunchtime. We can then decide on our next step into the unknown!" she said, and I laughed.

We found a café upstairs in the shopping complex. We made ourselves comfortable at a table ad ordered toasted cheese sandwiches and a pot of tea.

We chatted about the freedom we were enjoying, hoping that it was how our future would be. After lunch, we couldn't be bothered to do any more shopping, so Jill decided that we'd go back to the house and have one of our lovely walks together.

When we got back to Cliff House, I grabbed my binoculars from my car and then we told the driver where we were going to walk. We set off up a path that led to another part of the cliffs, through shrubs in flower that gave off a delightful perfume. The sun was very warm, and it was good that we were equipped with sunhats and sunglasses. I asked Jill if she was enjoying the day and whether she was feeling more relaxed now.

"Yes," she said, "I actually feel normal."

We found a rock in the shade to serve as a seat. It wasn't very comfortable, but it was good enough for a few minutes. Jill was using my binoculars to look out to sea. I told her that I was just going to walk on a bit, to the area where I'd seen a person lying down and using binoculars. I found a flattened area about the length of a person of medium height. I rang Sue on my mobile and told her. She told me not to worry as her agents would be checking the area regularly. I returned to Jill. I told her what I'd seen and about my conversation with Sue. Then we set off once again along the cliff top, and did a right turn to bring us back to the house. We walked across the lawn and then sat on a wooden seat where we enjoyed admiring the flowers and breathing in the scent-filled air.

The butler came out and offered us tea, to which we said a

resounding "yes". The butler brought out a small table and then a tray with tea.

"What are we doing tonight?" Jill asked, and I noticed that she used "we", and I smiled.

"We could dine at the hotel," I suggested, "unless you have other ideas."

"No, that's perfect," Jill replied "I don't want to be too late tonight as I am feeling a little tired. It's been a hard week."

After another brief walk around Cliff House's gardens, I decided it was time to go back to the hotel. Back on my balcony, I sat thinking positive thoughts about our future together. Then I had a shower and got ready for dinner with Jill.

When I walked into the restaurant, the waiter took me to a table for four near the window. I had not been seated long when Jill came in looking gorgeous and causing heads to turn as she walked towards me. I stood up and kissed her on the cheek. She sat opposite me and smiled the smile that always turned me to jelly.

"I thought I ought to invite Bill," she said, "but he has a meeting."

"Good," I said, "I want you to myself!"

She laughed.

We enjoyed wine and steak while being serenaded by the romantic music that was playing in the restaurant. We both commented on how nice it was to enjoy a romantic meal on our own and how we hoped there would be plenty more like this in our future.

Some other couples were dancing to the music, so we joined them for a couple of slow dances.

"I'm so sorry, Ray, but I feel exhausted," Jill said, as we walked back to our table. I'll have to give dessert and coffee a miss and head home."

"Please don't worry," I replied, "it has been a hectic few days."

Jill phoned her driver while I settled the bill. We walked to the front entrance, and the Jag was waiting at the door for her.

She kissed me and said goodnight, got in the car, waved, and it set off. I was rather tired too, so I retired for the night.

I woke up early the next day, showered, got dressed and had breakfast. It was the day of the festival, and I hoped that this was going to be a special day. It had been arranged that Jill and I would go in the Range Rover car accompanied by two bodyguards. The festival was starting at 2 pm and was being held about twenty-five miles away from my hotel, at a big manor house with extensive grounds. I had been told that it had been a great success last time they held it, and in the present political climate, I felt it would be a good boost to the economy.

Bill had got Mike a ticket to the VIP quarters, where Jill, Bill, Sue and I would be eating, drinking and meeting the dignitaries as they appeared. Jill and I were looking forward to it. I decided to go for a drive as I had plenty of time before we had to leave for the festival. I headed off down the coast road, then cut inland a few miles and stopped at a roadside café. I had just ordered a cup of tea when a voice suddenly said, "Hi Ray!"

I turned around. It was Dec, the client I had dined with a few nights previously. We shook hands, and he told me that he was on his way to meet a client in Overstrand and had just stopped for a drink. We chatted for a few minutes before I told him that I needed to get back to my hotel. "You have my number, if you need me," I said, and then left.

CHAPTER 14

End of the Adventure

After packing a few bits and bobs into my shoulder bag, I got dressed in a blue shirt with tie, trousers and a blazer. I then drove over to Cliff House and parked near the Jag, Range Rover and a blue Opal car.

Jill greeted me at the door with a quick kiss. She looked ravishing in her cream-coloured dress and shoes to match. She also looked efficient and fabulously wealthy. Inside, was Sue, who looked very glamorous, and who was accompanied by a smart-looking agent. She reminded us to make sure our two bodyguards were kept informed where we were at all times, and got us to programme a number into our mobiles that we could use to call for immediate help.

Bill got into the Jag with a driver, Sue got into the Opel with her agent driving, and Jill and I got into the Range Rover with our two bodyguards. We set off to the "Festival."

We soon arrived at the manor and were dropped off with Sue and a bodyguard While our drivers parked the cars.

We entered the manor and were shown to the main area where the opening ceremony would take place, and shown to our seats ready to watch who came in and play "who's who"!

There were film stars, barons and baronets, ambassadors, high ranking industrialists, plus people who had done volunteer work for the people of the UK and abroad.

Jill was very excited and kept pointing out people to me she recognised, and, since she had been out of circulation for a while, I was able to point out some people she didn't know or recognise. Soon the opening ceremony began and speeches made. A minister opened it, and everyone went into the room to enjoy refreshments. The idea was to circulate, and Bill introduced us to people as friends. Luckily, I did see and speak to one or two who I knew from my own business dealings, and Jill kept a low profile, remaining very close to me.

"Do you want a snack," I said to Jill, "if so, we can get one each and get a table to sit at."

She nodded 'yes', so I guided her to the table of food to help herself. We then found a table and a waiter brought drink. We relaxed and just acknowledged people as they passed by our table. All of a sudden, I spotted Mike and stood up and put my arm in the air for him to see, which he did and came over. I introduced Jill, and they shook hands.

"I've heard so much about you from Ray," Mike said to Jill.

Jill smiled, "All good, I hope!"

"Of course!"

"He can be such a charmer!" I laughed.

Sue walked near our table, and Mile beckoned her over, "How about you and me go get some food," he said to her, "and then we can all go together around the exhibition. What do you two think?" he turned to Jill and me.

"Good idea," Jill and I said in unison.

Mike and Sue went off to get food and were back in just a few minutes. We made small talk while they ate. Then, we all stood up, Sue spoke into her wrist, and we set off around the exhibition.

We all enjoyed looking at the new range of cars on show, and took turns in sitting in them. There were all sorts of stalls, including ones for IT, artwork and building companies. I noticed Bill in conversation at one of the building ones. We went past stalls for the Navy, Army and Air force, and Mike and I met an old pal on one of them, a man we hadn't seen in years: Rob Bowen, who was now wearing a captain's commando uniform. We congratulated him on his promotion and had a few words with him. Jill and Sue seemed to be enjoying themselves, and we all had a laugh on an IT stall, trying to do a game.

We came upon a marquee where drinks were being served, so we sat down and ordered tea.

"Look over there to the right," Sue gestured with her eyes, "there are a lot of ambassadors and embassy staff there, rubbing shoulders with other ambassadors and staff. They're all pretending to be friendly," she laughed, "and, there, on the far right is my counterpart in the Russian embassy, standing with two others."

We all looked over, and I felt Jill stiffen beside me as a woman standing with the Russians seemed to notice us. She looked carefully at us, then waved and started to walk towards us.

"She's an old college friend!" Jill gasped.

"Just bluff it out," Sue said quickly.

"Yulia, isn't it?" The woman said to Jill as she arrived at our table. She had a slight accent.

"No, you're mistaken," I said.

"Oh, I'm sorry," she said, "apart from the hair colour, you look very much like someone I went to college with."

"Sorry," Jill said politely, "but I didn't actually go to college, and my name's not Yulia."

"Oh dear, I'm so very sorry," the woman said, "I could have sworn you were her." She walked back to the others and, no doubt, fed back to them what had happened.

"My people are on the way," Sue said to us, "and when they get here, let's slowly and casually walk back to the main hall, as if nothing untoward has happened."

Two agents turned up, but stood back a bit so that we noticed them, but they weren't too obvious. We all stood up and followed Sue's instructions. I was holding Jill's hand, which was shaking. I looked over at the Russian woman, she was talking to two men who were looking over at Jill. In a whisper, I mentioned it to Mike, who nodded.

On our arrival back in the main hall, Sue sent a message to Bill's bodyguard to update him and to tell him to make sure he and Bill kept their distance. Sue asked the two agents who were following us to keep an eye out for anyone tailing us.

Bill phoned Sue, and I heard him say, "Does this mean what I think it does, Sue?"

"Yes," she replied, "Jill's cover is blown, and she certainly cannot go back to Cliff House. Your cover may well be blown too. My supervisor will insist on a relocation and new names for you both now. I am sorry to say that this will be the end of the road as far as Cliff House is concerned."

Sue finished her conversation with Bill and then excused herself to ring her department. She was gone for just a few minutes, and on her return, she took me, Jill and Mike into another room and explained the situation.

"Jill cannot go back to the house," she said, "We've arranged for a helicopter to land nearby to take you away, Jill. They can't follow you that way."

Jill burst into tears, and I pulled her close, trying to comfort her.

I overheard Mike say to Sue in a low voice, "I think they will both take this badly, they are very much involved."

"Yes, I know," she said, "but I have to think about what's best for Jill and Bill."

Suddenly, one of the bodyguards hurried into the room.

"The two men who were with the Russian lady are just outside the door and have been asking questions about Jill," he said.

Mike wasn't quick enough to stop me as I ran to the door and pulled it open. One of the Russians was lurking by the door, and I couldn't help myself, I punched him in the face. He ran off, holding his nose.

"Now you've done it!" Mike shouted at me, "they will be certain they are right now." "I'm sorry, but these foreign agents are ruining Jill's life," I said, "and it's not right that anyone living in this country should live in fear of foreign agents!"

"Ray, your rash action has given them the answer they were looking for, though," he said gently, and I slumped down on a nearby chair, my head in my hands.

"I'll take you back to the hotel in my car," he said, "I'm afraid that Sue will already have spirited Jill and Bill away by now."

"I'll never see her again, will I?" I whispered.

Mike put his arm around my shoulder, "I'm sorry, old man, I'm sorry."

We got into Mike's car and headed off out of the car park, Mike keeping an eye on his mirrors to check that we weren't being tailed, and avoiding the normal route.

Finally, we were back at the hotel.

We had driven in silence but now I spoke, "It's a good thing I shall be going home tomorrow afternoon,"

"Yes," Mike said, "Look, Ray, it's going to take some time to get over this, but at least Jill is safe, and I'm sure she will never forget you."

"I would have liked to have been able to say goodbye," I commented.

Mike sighed, "Sue did the right thing, Ray. She had to remove them from the situation urgently."

I just nodded.

We entered reception, and Mike booked a room for the night.

I couldn't bear an evening of being on my balcony and thinking about Jill, so I suggested we go out to the Oyster Duck for some entertainment. Mike agreed, and I asked the receptionist to book a taxi for us for 6.45 pm and to book a table at the Oyster Duck.

"I have something that you'll want to read," Mike said, and we went back to his room. He poured us both a gin and tonic from the mini bar, and we went out on his balcony. Mike handed me a folder, and I opened it and started reading. It was a file on Bill and Jill Stevens. Mike had found out a great deal about them.

Bill had been the head of a firm who dealt in property - commercial buildings and defence property, and other secret properties - and he had become very wealthy through doing this, despite communism. His company had dealt with the Kremlin departments, including the KGB on certain items that were classed as secret. Bill had been secretly moving his wealth overseas for a number of years and grooming a couple of board members to take over his business in the future. He had diversified and invested in property outside of Russia, including in the UK, and by the time he had decided to leave Russia, he was very well prepared to do so financially. However, he had realised that the KGB, or the FBS, would not take kindly to his decision, and could cause him problems.

He also knew that if he applied for asylum in the UK, the Russians could try to use his sister to get him back. Fortunately, his sister was not happy with her life, and so was happy to leave with him. They knew that they had to put the FBS off the scent, and the UK authorities helped them by making it look like the siblings had been killed in a car accident in Germany.

Bill had gone through cosmetic surgery, but Jill had refused, believing that it was Bill that the Russians were really after, and him they knew well. Then they were put under the protection of MI5.

Reading the file made me understand just how difficult Jill's position had been. It was all so sad. I gave the file back to Mike, thanked him, and retired to my room.

I had just entered my room when my mobile rang. It was Jill.

"I have to be quick, but I just wanted to say that I am so very sorry that things turned out this way, Ray," she said with a catch in her voice, "and I want you to know I love you, and I shall never ever forget you."

"And I won't forget you," I said, "I love you."

"I must go," she said, and hung up.

I had a shower and got ready to go out, although I certainly was not in the mood. I had to keep busy though and I was grateful to Mike for being there for me at this time.

I went down to reception, where Mike was standing, waiting for me.

"The taxi's here," he said.

The journey was uneventful, and we were soon at the Oyster Duck. A waiter showed us to our table, the same one we'd sat at before, and took our drinks order.

We declined starters, and then the waiter came back with a bottle of wine, and Mike ordered a steak while I ordered a salmon salad. I poured us a glass of wine each, and we clinked our glasses.

"To us," said Mike, and I repeated the words after him.

"Thank you for coming out with me tonight," I said, "but I'm not sure I'm very good company."

He smiled sadly.

We ate our meals in near-total silence, concentrating on eating.

At a manor house near London, Popov was listening to the agent in charge of the blond woman case, who was updating him on the day's events.

"Unfortunately, she disappeared before we could do anything," the agent said, "MI5 must have got her out of there."

Popov sighed.

"But," the agent went on, we did follow a man that was with her at the festival and a man that our agents recognised from before. He was with another man, and it looks like they're staying at the Whitehouse Hotel. It's not far from a property called Cliff House, where a helicopter landed this afternoon and where that has been lots of coming and going, with furniture and possessions being moved."

"I told you it stinks of MI5," said Popov, "and we need agents to watch the house and some others to keep an eye on the man. If anyone sees the woman, then she is to be eliminated without pause or question. Understand?"

"Understood, sir.." The agent said, and left the room.

Popov was annoyed. Why had he been stupid enough to believe that it was not the blond woman when they had first spotted her?

Sue had arranged for Jill and Bill to be taken away by helicopter, so that nobody could follow them, and had asked the siblings for a list of items they needed, things she'd get agents to take from their home and then send on when things had calmed down.

"We'll have to be extra vigilant," she told her agents, "Popov is not going to be happy that we pulled the wool over his eyes, or that Ray attacked one of his agents. He'll be determined to get to Bill and Jill. Please make sure that all agents are armed," she added.

Sue thought about the phone call she'd had with Ray about the person he saw using binoculars in the long grass on the cliff top near Cliff House. She decided to send agents to that area too, just in case. Ray and Mike were enjoying the entertainment, and Ray was even joining in with some of the songs. The wine had mellowed the two men and made Ray put his problems to one side for a while.

The singer could see that the two men were enjoying her act and so played up to them. She sang a couple of songs directly to them, and they enjoyed that. They clapped and whistled when she stopped for an interval and left the stage.

"Alcohol is not the answer, but it does make things seem a little better," Ray said to Mike, his voice slightly slurred, and then he told Mike about Jill calling him.

"I'm surprised Sue let her do that!" Mike gasped, "or perhaps Jill did it behind Sue's back. It's a stupid and dangerous thing to do when calls can be traced easily enough, and the Russians may even have put a contract out on her now that she has been properly recognised."

"A contract?" I asked, frowning.

"Yes," said Mike, "I think you know what I mean."

"She's important enough to do that?" Suddenly I was stone-cold sober.

"Yes," Mike replied, "so if she tries to make contact with you again then you need to tell her not to do it again, and hang up as soon as you can."

The singer came on again, and we both enjoyed it, but by the time she had finished, we were more than ready to go back to the hotel. In reception, we shook hands and said goodnight, then I went up to my room and flopped into bed.

I met Mike for breakfast, both of us feeling a little worse for wear, and made small talk over our food. After we had finished, Mike explained that he'd got some calls to make before he checked out: "But remember that I am always here for you," he said, as we shook hands. I told him that I was going for a walk along the beach to clear the cobwebs, but wished him well for his journey.

I walked out of reception and down the path to the beach, where I decided to walk along the sea's edge, breathing in the bracing sea air. There was no one about, and the only sound was the surf breaking on the sand. I couldn't help but look towards the steps up to Cliff House, and I was surprised to see Jill waving at me and shouting my name. She started running down the steps, and I broke into a run

We met at the bottom, hugging and kissing, then she let go of me and stood back to look me in the eyes. Suddenly, I heard the crack of a rifle and Jill fell to the ground. She'd been shot in the head. I dropped to the ground and cradled her head, bursting into tears, and then Sue and Mike were at my side.

"She's gone," Mike said after checking Jill's neck and wrist for a pulse, "I'm so sorry, Ray," he put a hand on my shoulder.

"The bastard must be on the cliff top," I muttered.

Sue ran back towards the steps while speaking into her wrist.

There were several more shots and then silence. I just knelt there with Jill, not even considering whether I was in any danger

The sniper had arrived early to make sure he had a good position in the high grass on the cliff top. There may just be a chance that MI5 would be careless and let the woman come back to the house for some items.

He had brought a flask and had on a full camouflage outfit, making him difficult to spot in the grass. He had his high powered rifle with a scope, and other items to make a pinpoint shot. He was a patient man, and eventually he saw people moving about near the house and heard several cars arrive, and people chatting. He lay there in silence, unmoving and keeping an eye out. Through his scope, he noticed a man walking on the sand and looking out to sea. Then, he heard a raised voices and a dark-haired woman ran to the steps that led down to the beach, She shouted and waved her arm, and the man on the beach turned around and started to run towards her. She ran down the steps as fast as she could, and the couple met at the bottom of the steps. They embraced. The sniper was positive that it was the woman he had been ordered to eliminate. He took careful aim as the woman stepped back. It was a good shot. The woman crumpled to the ground, and the sniper quickly gathered his things together to make his exit. Suddenly, he saw three men running towards him on the cliff top. All three were armed with pistols at the ready. Damn, he thought, as he set off running. The three men split up to cover all sides and cut him off.

"Freeze, or I'll shoot," said one with his pistol trained on him. There was nowhere to go, and his rifle had been dismantled and packed away. But he had a pistol in a holster, so he went for that. Before he could reach it, a shot rang out, and he fell to the ground.

"He's dead," said the MI5 agent to the others, prodding the sniper with his foot.

I was in a daze. Somebody took Jill's body out of my arms and I couldn't do anything, I couldn't react. Somehow, Mike got me back to my room and I was sipping hot tea laced with brandy. It seemed to revive me a bit.

"Where's Jill?" I asked.

Mike told me that MI5 had taken her away and that there were lots of things to sort out, "but they will treat her with respect," he added, putting a hand on my shoulder again.

There was a soft knock on the door, and Mike let Sue in. She looked pale.

"Will there be a funeral?" I asked, "Will I be able to go?"

Sue shook her head sadly, "I'm sorry, Ray, we need to make it so that Jill never existed. She was never here..." she trailed off.

"I always thought that Bill was 'the man who never was', but it was Jill who they got to in the end." I was weeping now.

"The gunman is dead, though, if that helps in any way," Sue said.

I gave Sue some money, asking for her to get some flowers to be put with Jill's remains, wherever they would go. "Please could you add a card just saying 'you are with me forever, Love Ray," I added.

Sue nodded with understanding, "Of course, she would never have forgotten you, you know, and I'll never forget you either, Ray," she shook my hand, "Good luck, but this never happened, you never met the Stevens on this holiday, OK?"

I nodded, and she walked out of the door.

"She's taking this badly too, you know," said Mike, " she thinks she failed Jill."

I simply nodded.

A bit later, after some more tea and brandy, I'd come out of my shock and anger and grief was hitting me. I couldn't quite get to grips with the idea that I'd never see Jill again. My usual way of dealing with things was to keep busy, to immerse myself in my work. I decided that I needed to get back to work, I had to leave. I told Mike.

"Well, Ray, we have been through all sorts together in the forces, and I know we can come through this," he said, "you're a strong man, so come on, marine, you can do this."

He knew that empty platitudes wouldn't help, so didn't carry on. He excused himself, then, saying that he'd got some urgent calls to make. He patted me heavily on the back, and I was able to joke about his strength. Suddenly, we were back to our usual banter, and just for a minute, all seemed normal. We shook hands and made our farewells.

I had a lot to get right in my mind, and I knew it would take a few days before I did, but getting back home and dealing with everyday problems would help me on my journey with grief. I had never known a woman like Jill, a love like that, and it would not be an easy journey. Had it always been at the back of our minds that things could end like this? I asked myself. Perhaps so. As the saying went, better to have loved and lost, than never to have loved at all. The pain was unbearable, but I would not have missed a single minute of the last few days. The pain came from great love.

To escape my gloomy thoughts, I decided to check out and go home. I paid my bill and thanked the staff for their service. "Sir, there's a message for you," the receptionist said as she gave me my receipt. She handed me a note.

I carried my luggage to my car, put it in the boot, sat in the driver's seat and opened the folded piece of paper:

"Please get in contact, Ray, I need help! Dec."

I started the engine and drove slowly down to the main road. Then I pulled over. Should I call him now? I thought. The message was mysterious, a whole new adventure, perhaps…